Emma —

With this ring…

Heritage Series – Volume III

Susan Diane Black Blackmon

Library of Congress Control Number: 2024926736

Emma - With this ring…

– Heritage Series – Volume III

by *Susan Diane Black Blackmon.*

Paperback ISBN: 978-1-959980-06-3

Hardcover ISBN: 978-1-959980-05-6

Ebook ISBN: 978-1-959980-07-0

Independently published by Susan Diane Black Blackmon, Whispers from the Past.....™, 767 Mountain Top Loop, Graham, Texas, USA, 76450

www.susanblackmon.com

www.whispersfromthepast.net

I dedicate this story to my MamMaw, Alta Leona Driver. She spent countless hours sharing her knowledge of our family history; I am eternally grateful for that.

About the Author

In 1976, I fell in love with genealogy. I have my eighth-grade History teacher to thank for that. She assigned an auto-bio-graphical project requiring us to complete a pedigree chart. "The Tale of the Beautiful Princess - Or Everything You Always Wanted to Know About Me, But Were Afraid to Ask" resulted in two A+ grades.

Over the next forty-six years, I amassed a collection of thousands of photographs and documents related to my family heritage. Most importantly,

I spent countless hours listening to my MamMaw (grandmother) and my great-aunt tell stories about my ancestors.

I compiled several genealogy books and "published them" at the local print shop. In 2015, I published my first set of books through Amazon and my second set in 2017.

In September of 2022, I completed a project that had been the dream of a cousin. He had always wanted to write a book based on Civil War letters he inherited from his great-grandmother by way of an aunt. The letters and memorabilia "lived" in a pillowcase inside a chair cushion for many years. My cousin passed away before he could realize his dream, and I had the honor of presenting these 158-year-old treasures in a format that allowed the entire family to enjoy them. Hot on the heels of publishing this work came my sixtieth birthday.

Turning sixty may have been the reason I allowed my older sister to shove me out of my wheelhouse of genealogy and into writing a work of Historical fiction. Older sisters can be pretty bossy, and this one has a sharp stick that she likes to poke me with, metaphorically.

She kept "encouraging" me to try my hand at writing a book. I intended to write a short story based on our great-grandmother and the events in her life. I had planned on a handful of pages to satisfy my sister, and it would be back to my next genealogy project. Two weeks later, I presented her with a 264-page rough draft of *Emma*. She read it, insisted I let other family members and friends read it, and the next thing you know, here we are with the third in a series of books rooted in family history and interwoven with imagination.

I hope you enjoy Emma's latest adventures!

Table of Contents

Prologue 1

Chapter 1 9

Chapter 2 17

Chapter 3 27

Chapter 4 39

Chapter 5 47

Chapter 6 59

Chapter 7 69

Chapter 8 77

Chapter 9 89

Chapter 10 105

Chapter 11 115

Chapter 12 121

Chapter 13 129

Chapter 14 141

Chapter 15 155

Chapter 16 163

Chapter 17 173

Chapter 18 187

Chapter 19 197

Chapter 20 205

Chapter 21 211

Chapter 22 225

Chapter 23 237

Chapter 24 247

Epilogue 253

Characters 261

Coconut Cream Cake 269

Coconut Cream Filling... 271

Coconut Butter Frosting 273

Other Titles Available 275

Illustrations 291

Prologue

1901 Liberty Grove, Texas –

Emma held her breath, willing her heart not to beat so loudly. She calmed herself, deciding the rustling noise that had frightened her must have been a rabbit. Careful not to go in a straight line, she stepped on stones to avoid leaving footprints and started walking again. Freedom was too close to make a foolish mistake and get caught now.

Papa had dogged her every step the past few days. That she had managed to slip away was a miracle. Papa would raise a ruckus the minute he noticed she was gone. He had become *so* demanding, and often Emma felt she could not breathe and might never be free again.

The changes of the past few months swirled through her mind. Emma would never understand why Papa had allowed her stepmother, Matilda, to treat his children so poorly. The woman had detested them from the day she entered the house. She had made life miserable for all of them, including her daughters. As the older children had married and moved away, Matilda had focused her cruelty on Emma and her younger sister, Ida. The girls had lived in fear of the next hateful outburst from the woman.

A year had passed since Emma had taken the train to visit her sister, Betsy, in Caseyville. While she was away, a fire destroyed their childhood home, seriously injuring her papa and resulting in Matilda's death. Emma had come back to Liberty Grove to care for Papa, expecting a short stay before returning to her new life, and Charley, the man who had asked to marry her and whom she loved dearly.

Gingerly, she picked her way down the creek bank, fighting the urge to run when she heard the creek's rushing water. She would be at the tree that guarded her most precious secrets in only a few more feet.

Years earlier, Emma had picked the spot under the towering live oak to hide the treasures she had kept as a little girl. She had chosen this spot, knowing Matilda would never walk to the creek and because it was far enough off the path that no one else would stumble across it.

She had to be especially careful to conceal her tracks today. It would never do for Papa to find out what she was hiding.

Emma withdrew the letter from the pocket of her apron - the paper showed wear from all the times she had read and tucked it away.

27 July 1901

My Dearest Emma,

Our time apart is ending. I will arrive on the one o'clock train on Saturday, August 11th.

Dearest, please exercise caution until I arrive to take you home. Know that I will not rest until we are together. I do not understand why your pa has decided to object to our marriage, but rest assured, we _will_ be married.

Until I look upon your lovely face once more, I remain affectionately yours,

Charley.

Emma folded the letter and held it to her bosom. Charley would be here soon, and all would be right with her world. She knelt, pushing aside the stones and moss that protected her secrets, and lifted a bundle from the earth. Her hands shook as she brushed the loose dirt from the ducking and prayed that it had kept out the moisture. She struggled to untie the string that bound it. Emma glanced around, deciding she was safe, and removed the treasures of the young woman she had become.

Papa had searched her room after she told him she was going back to Caseyville. The wrinkled pages of Charley's letters were evidence of his anger. She caressed them, remembering every word that Charley had written to her. After wrapping the missives in the waterproof ducking, she briefly held the package to her lips and whispered, "Soon, my love." Then, she returned them to their hiding place, carefully smoothing the moss and leaves that concealed them.

When she slipped back through the kitchen door, she heard Papa say, "That girl is up to no good! I don't care what you say. She *is* hiding something, and I intend to find out what it is."

Emma's heart faltered; *had she been careless?* She stepped into the main room, hoping she did not look guilty.

Chapter 1

Cleaning up after the fire had been an overwhelming job. Along with the flood of memories that came every time she went to the old homeplace, the summer heat and the ash covering everything quickly took their toll on Emma.

The most dangerous debris had been cleared away, leaving a soot-covered mess for Emma to sift through. At this moment, she wished a large hole would open and swallow it all, herself included. Each time she felt that way, she stumbled across a precious item that had somehow survived the hungry flames.

 Just this morning, she had found Momma's silver thimble and the China doll that Ida had gotten for her first birthday. Buried in ash, Emma wondered how the poor doll had survived with only a small burn on the hem of her dress. It was finding these things that kept her going.

As her hands sorted through the wreckage, Emma recalled the events leading up to this day. The previous March, she had turned sixteen, and Papa had sent her to visit her family in Caseyville. On her first evening there, she met Charley. After getting off to a rocky start, Charley declared his intentions for her at a church social. He bid twenty dollars, an outrageous amount, for the opportunity to share the box lunch she had prepared. It wasn't long before they had fallen in love. He had asked her to marry him the night of the fire and had given her a cameo. Those days now seemed a lifetime ago.

The fire that had destroyed her childhood home and resulted in her stepmother Matilda's death was only one of the changes in her life. After fourteen years of anger and reproach, Papa reconciled with her grandparents, Ma and Grandpa George. Ma had begged Papa to live with them after the fire, hoping to make up for their time apart. Papa would not hear of it, insisting it would burden the older couple and that it was time for him to provide his girls with a real home.

With Papa rebuilding, Emma had stayed longer than she had planned. Someone had to sort through the rubble, and it had fallen to her. She didn't mind helping, but she often felt uneasy whenever Papa talked about doing things for "his girls." Emma gently reminded him that she would leave for Caseyville soon, but she wasn't sure whether he understood and accepted that she was going.

Her thoughts returned to Charley. The first day she returned to the burned-out house had been full of surprises and small miracles. Hoping to make sense of the tragedy, she had stared through a broken window, watching ash swirl in the breeze. The acrid smell of the burnt wood had made her stomach knot, thinking of what she could have lost. She was drawn into the house and wrestled with the door, hanging by a single hinge. When the door frame had given way, she had landed in the middle of the rubble. Filthy and breathless, she had been shocked to see the likeness of her parents hanging above the stone fireplace. In awe, she slowly approached their portrait. Suddenly, strong masculine hands gripped her arms. Preparing to defend herself, she spun around to find it was *her* Charley. She had not known that he was coming to Liberty Grove, and she chuckled to herself, remembering that the mere sight of him had filled her with joy.

When would she see Charley again? As the lonely days had turned to weeks since she had seen him last, she had begun to worry that it had all been a dream. When she began to fret, she would touch the cameo at her throat, and a feeling of calm would surround her. Charley *was* real, and in time, they would be together again.

Emma's stomach grumbled, and she was shocked at how late it had become. She loaded her day's finds in the wagon, hitched the horse, and headed to Ma's. The trip wasn't long, just enough time to settle her mind. The tragic fire seemed to have completely healed the rift between Papa and Ma. Emma did not remember the horrible scene at her momma's burial when Papa, in his grief, had condemned Ma for Jane's death. Even though her grandparents lived nearby, they had not been a part of her life until *after* the fire. Emma marveled at how strange it was that tragedy could either drive a family apart or draw them together.

Papa was getting stronger every day, and Ma had been such a blessing in caring for him. She fixed him thick broths and hearty stews and saw to his bandaged arm. They had settled into a comfortable routine at Ma and Grandpa George's. Papa's arm was healing nicely; he had a bit of stiffness in his fingers from the burns, but Ma made a salve for the damaged skin. She also made him squeeze a ball of rags, which would help strengthen his hand and keep the fingers from "locking down permanent-like."

Emma was not as concerned about Papa's hand as she was about his mind. The doctor had told them that Matilda had been poisoning him with arsenic, explaining why he had always seemed distracted. Once the poison was out of his blood, he had been better and more alert, but lately, he was slipping back into confusion. He would say the strangest things just when she thought the fog was clearing. Emma wouldn't be so concerned about this plan to re-build the house *if* she still lived at home. She had planned to stay long enough to ensure he was well on his way to being whole, but she was anxious to return to Caseyville and Charley.

Chapter 2

It had been two months since Emma had taken the train from Caseyville back to Liberty Grove; it felt like two years. She and Papa had been to the homesite to check on the progress of the new house. With the help of their neighbors, the walls were up, and the roof was in place. They would hang the doors and windows in about a week and finish the floor. Emma counted the days until Papa and Ida moved in, and she would be free to return home to Charley.

Emma had begun to feel more at ease over Papa and Ida living on the farm again. The Widow Key would cook and keep house during the week, and Papa had hired her son to help with chores. Ida would be able to continue her schooling, and on the weekends, she could prepare simple meals for them. Emma had been teaching her to bake pear pie, Papa's favorite, and other simple dishes. Ma told her that she would see that they didn't starve, and that Ida did not have more on her young shoulders than she could bear. It made Emma happy that although Ida was not Ma's blood relation, she and Grandpa George loved the young girl as their own.

Papa's voice interrupted her thoughts: "I'll need you to help with furnishing the house. I know you were able to save bits and pieces, but plenty will need replacing." Emma had already planned to help, and she and Ma had been busy sewing sheets and towels. The ladies at the church had been more than generous with quilts and cookware. Emma mentally reviewed their needs, and only one or two items remained. Curtains would be ready by the end of the week, and Ma had almost finished a rag rug for Ida's room. Other than minor details, Emma thought everything was in order. She patted Papa's knee. "Of course, Papa, whatever you need."

The rain was not what anyone expected. Emma began to think they should consider building an ark. The creek between Ma's and Papa's farm had risen so much that the bridge was washed out. Thankfully, Papa's hired hand would look after the animals he had moved back to the barn. Work on the house came to a halt as the roads were impassable. Two weeks passed, and there was not a cloudless sky in sight. Emma began to fret. With the bridge out, she could not get to town to telegraph Charley that she would be delayed. Although he was not expecting her for another week, the rain, the bridge repair, and the time it would take to finish the house would delay Emma for at least another month.

The water receded, the roads dried, and the men repaired the bridge.

Moving day was upon them, and Ida was dancing with excitement. Papa had bought her a new bed with a soft feather mattress. The curtains she had helped to sew and had embroidered with tiny purple and yellow flowers fluttered in the breeze from the open window in her room. The gaily colored rug that Ma had sewn for her now lay on the floor, and each time her bare feet touched its softness, she felt as if Ma was hugging her. Ida had never been happier. She had a beautiful room that was all hers, and Papa said she could invite her friends over after school. Her mother had never allowed her to have visitors. Ida knew she should be sad that Mother had died, but she was not. Her mother had always been unkind to her, and she did not remember Matilda ever saying, "I love you." or hugging her as Ma did. Ida was secretly thankful that Mother was not here to spoil this day.

Emma entered Ida's room and smiled at the young girl's obvious pleasure. She brought a neatly wrapped package from behind her back and handed it to her younger sister. Ida stared at it a moment before taking it in trembling hands. "What can this be?" As Ida removed the wrapping, she saw her doll; Ida thought Missie had burned in the fire. She got Missie for her first birthday; the *only* birthday present she had ever received. Ida lovingly cradled her baby, noticing the blue ribbon at the hem of her dress. "Her hem burned a bit; I thought the blue looked pretty with her eyes.," Emma said. Ida flung her arms around her sister and was so happy she felt her heart would burst.

Emma snuggled into the guest bed that evening, and every bone in her body was tired. The day had been long, but Papa and Ida finally settled into their new house. Emma had sent a telegram to Charley, letting him know she planned to be on the train this coming Friday. She would return to her sister, Betsy's, in time to help her prepare for Thanksgiving. Knowing that Ma would look after Ida and Papa gave her a sense of comfort. She did not think she would be able to leave otherwise. Emma ran down the list of things she wanted to do before she left. She planned to make one more trip to the mercantile to ensure that Papa and Ida had everything they needed, and she wanted to bake a pear pie for their last supper together. She planned to talk to the woman Papa had hired and make sure she would contact Ma or send word if Papa needed anything. She was still worried about him.

His hand and arm were healed entirely. He had gained weight, and the dark, thick patches of skin, a tell-tale sign of Matilda's poisoning, were almost gone. Even his beard was less scraggly. But it was his mind that worried her. Sometimes, he mistook her for her mother, Jane. Emma knew she looked very much like her momma, but this was different. It was as if Papa thought she *was* Jane. She consoled herself with Doctor Perkins' assurances that it was just the aftereffects of the poison and that, in time, his mind would clear.

Truthfully, it wasn't just that he sometimes confused her with her momma; he didn't seem to grasp that she no longer lived with him and Ida, that she was only visiting and would be leaving soon to return to Caseyville. The bed she lay in was witness to that. Emma had told Papa repeatedly that he did not need to build her a room; she could stay with Ma or her sister, Luella. Papa had insisted that she needed a room of her own, and rather than argue and upset him, Emma had picked out a bed and chest and dutifully sewn linens and curtains to decorate the room. It *was* a pretty room, and the bed was comfortable, nicer than anything they had growing up.

Emma pushed away her misgivings about Papa. As she drifted to sleep, she thought of her upcoming train ride and how different it would be from her other trips. She was excited to make the trip this time, knowing Charley would be waiting for her at the station.

Chapter 3

Friday morning, Emma was awake before the sun came up. She was not even sure she had slept. Supper the night before had been an emotional time. As excited as she was to be on her way home to Charley, she dreaded leaving her family here. Seeing her sister, Etta, her husband, James, and their children had been lovely. Although Etta was meeting Ma for the first time, it was as if they had known and loved each other their whole lives. Etta had promised her to look in on Papa and Ida often. Papa with his grandchildren on his lap was a happy sight. When he and Ida visited Caseyville, he would meet the rest of the little ones. Everyone stayed until the wee hours, hating to go home, not knowing when they would be together again.

Emma crept from her bed, not wanting to wake the household. She padded softly to the kitchen to stir the fire and set the coffee to boil. As she passed her father's door, he moaned. Thinking he must be dreaming, she continued to the kitchen but stopped when she heard his racking cough.

Papa was burning up. Emma called out for Ida; she needed the child to sit with him while she brewed the willow bark tea Ma had taught her to make. Despite his violent coughing, the girls managed to get the sips of the tea down his throat. Emma wanted to go for Doctor Perkins but hated leaving Ida alone with Papa. When the hired hand arrived, she sent him to fetch the doctor *and* Ma.

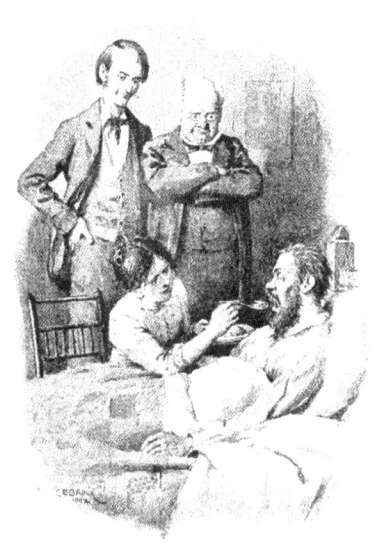

Papa had influenza. He was out of his head with a fever, and that horrible cough showed he had pneumonia. Doctor Perkins and his young assistant said there was nothing to do but wait and pray. Ma arrived just after the doctor had left. She brought her case of herbal remedies. Ma had learned how to use plants for healing from Manita and Topsana, the Indian women she had known when she lived in Gabriel Mills. The women carried Papa's bed into the main room by the fire, and Ma went to work.

Ida had the fire blazing. Ma said they needed to sweat the disease out of him. She set a kettle over the fire, and they constructed a tent over his bed to trap the steam. Ma brewed pleurisy root tea and fed him a spoonful at a time. Each time he swallowed, he would cough until he convulsed. Emma was terrified Papa would die from it, but Ma reassured her that the tea would clear his lungs. They sent Ida to the kitchen to prepare a bone broth. Ben needed nourishment to fight the fever, and Ida was upset seeing him so ill. Ma rummaged in her case and added something to the steaming kettle. "Snakeweed helps the cough too." They spent the next hours feeding the fire and the kettle, struggling to get the

tea and broth down Papa's throat between the horrible coughing spells.

It was well after midnight when Ma
shooed Emma to bed. Emma argued
that she should stay with Papa and let
Ma rest, but Ma would not hear of it.
Emma looked in on Ida, who had fallen
asleep across her bed without undress-
ing. Emma pulled a quilt over the girl
and slipped from the room to avoid dis-
turbing her.

She sat on the side of her bed, head
in her hands, and prayed for her papa.
Ma insisted that he would live, but each
time she heard the coughing and wheez-
ing, a fresh wave of terror followed.
"God, please don't let Papa die. Please,
God, I *will* be a better daughter; just
please don't let him die."

When Emma woke, she had the oddest sensation that she wasn't where she was supposed to be. She opened one eye the tiniest bit against the sunlight streaming through the window. Why did her room at her sister Betsy's look like her room at Papa's house? How did Betsy know what it looked like, and why had she redone Emma's room? She lay there a minute longer, puzzled and disoriented, and then realized it was a dream. With a small cry, she sat up and moaned, "Charley!"

In all the worry over Papa, she had missed her train; worse, she had not sent a telegram to Charley. He would be beside himself with worry. What must he have thought when she was not on the train? Emma had to hurry, change clothes, and check on Papa. She

would ride into town and send a telegram to Charley as soon as possible.

When she entered the main room,
she was surprised to see that the tent
was gone. The room was still hot as
blazes, the kettle was still steaming, and
she could see her papa lying in the bed.
He seemed a bit delirious, but he was
not coughing. Grandpa George stood at
the stove, frying bacon and eggs, and
Ida softly hummed as she set the table
for breakfast.

"Good morning, my girl. How did
you rest? Your Ma is having a bit of a
lie down in Ida's room. Sit, sit, you
look famished." Emma started to protest; she needed to get to town and send
her message to Charley; he must be
frantic. Grandpa George continued,
"Don't be worrying about your young

man. I sent a telegram yesterday to let the folks know about your papa's illness. You had already gone to your bed when I got here last night, and I didn't want to disturb you with it." Emma sank into the chair, grateful for her grandfather.

After breakfast, Emma sat with her papa. She managed to coax him to take a few more small sips of broth and drink a cup of willow bark tea before Ma got up from her rest. Ma told Emma the coughing had eased during the night, and he had slept a little. She did not think he was entirely out of the woods, but he was much closer to the tree line than the night before.

The two women sat in the kitchen and enjoyed Ida's soft humming as she sat with Papa. After a bit, Ma said,

"That child has the voice and the heart of an angel. She is just a restful soul to have nearby. When your papa first brought Ida to me, she was so timid. She was helping me with the supper dishes one night and humming like she is now. I asked her the song's name, and the girl apologized for singing! That mother of hers had railed at her and called it caterwallin' or some such nonsense. I never thought I would say a child was better off without its ma, but that sweet girl most certainly is."

Emma thought about Matilda; her stepmother had mistreated Papa's children since she had walked through the door thirteen years earlier. She knew that it would be the Christian thing to feel bad because Matilda had died, yet she did not. It was sad that even Matilda's daughters, Etta and Ida, were not mourning her loss. Matilda had been an evil woman, much more so than they suspected. If she had not died that night, Papa would be lying next to Momma in the churchyard.

Papa drifted in and out of the fever for two more days. At times, he thrashed wildly, calling out for God to take him. As the fever cooled, he reached for an unseen hand and talked to his beloved Jane as if she stood before him.

Emma and Ma kept a vigil at his bedside. As the fever dried the moisture from the cool rag on his forehead, they tirelessly changed it for another, dampened with cold spring water. The sweat from his fever and the cold rags seemed to be working. By the end of the week, Papa was feeling well enough to sit up for short periods throughout the day.

Chapter 4

Thanksgiving was quickly approaching. Emma had planned to return to Caseyville long before then, but Papa's illness had been a setback. Still recovering from the aftereffects of the poison and the injuries from the fire, his bout with influenza and pneumonia had left him weak and unable to look after himself and Ida. Emma had sent letters to Charley and her sister, Betsy, explaining that she would need to stay awhile longer. She planned to be back with them for Christmas. Charlie had sent a telegram to let her know he would pray for them all 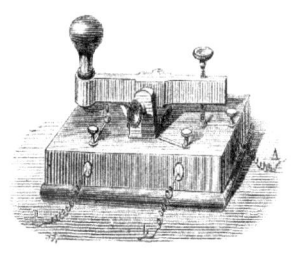 and that a letter would follow soon.

Emma and Ma planned Thanksgiving with her sisters, Luella, Etta, Jessie, and their families. Ida was beside herself with excitement. Matilda had never allowed them to have family gatherings; she hated cooking and refused to spend money on something she considered wasteful. While living with Betsy, Emma had started to realize all the things she and Ida had missed in their short lives. Ida had never had a birthday party or friends to play with. They had never had a Christmas tree or a Thanksgiving turkey. Emma was determined that this Thanksgiving would be the grandest celebration ever.

After two weeks, Papa was strong enough to sit in the sun on the porch for brief periods. While his body was healing, Emma *still* worried about his mind. If she was near, he was content. He would eat what they put in front of him, take his tonic without complaint, and rest whenever they told him to. Emma read to him each evening until he fell asleep. What worried Emma was that Papa did not want her out of his sight. She could barely go to the privy without him calling for her. Ma had gone home, and she and Ida were looking after Papa. Ida would sing for him and tell him stories about her day at school; he listened to her every word and told her repeatedly how proud he was of her. He allowed Ida to bring him his coffee and herbal tea that Ma had left, but *only* Emma could prepare it correctly.

Thanksgiving Day was lovely. The crisp fall air held a hint of wood smoke from the fireplace. The trees wore the most brilliant shades of red, orange, and yellow. The sky was clear, and the sun shone.   Horses grazed near the barn, hoping for treats from the tiny hands that petted their soft noses. The men had set up tables in the yard, and the women were busy arranging the steaming bowls and platters of food so the family could enjoy their feast.

The family that gathered totaled sixteen - Papa, Emma, and Ida. Ma and Grandpa George. Luella, Jackson, and their three boys, Riley, Ebb, and Sam. Etta, James, and their boys, Lee and Jim. Jessie and Henry. Jackson offered the blessing, and everyone agreed they had much to be thankful for this year. Papa and Ida were alive and living in the new house.   Ma and Grandpa George were welcome after too many years of Papa keeping them away. Etta was here with her family for the first time since she had married, enjoying time with her little sister, Ida. Emma looked at the faces around the tables, and her heart swelled with love. Another face filled her vision as she thought of her beloved Charley. She had hoped to be with him and the rest of her kin today. *Soon*, she thought.

Emma kept a close eye on Papa. He was enjoying having his children and grandbabies around him. His appetite was good, and he did not seem more tired than the rest. Emma thought that by the end of the week, it would be safe to send word to Charley that she would be on next Friday's train. She had been gone for more than four months! Emma had enjoyed her time with her Liberty Grove family, but it was time to go home and start her new life.

Charley had written to her about the farm where they would live. With Doc and Jim's help, he had cleared the site for their home. The lumber had arrived from the sawmill, and with the help of Emma's brothers and Charley's cousins, the outside walls were standing, and the roof was on. Charley hoped to have the windows and doors hung before Christmas. He told her how he wished she could have been there to see their little house grow, but he understood that her papa needed her. Emma cherished each letter that arrived from Caseyville. Her sisters kept her informed of the latest church and social news. She knew who was getting married or expecting a baby. They told her about their gardens and her nieces and nephews. Even Aunt Lucy sent her an occasional note. While their messages did ease her missing them, she was never wholly free of the longing to be with them.

On the Monday after Thanksgiving, Emma told Papa and Ida that she planned to take the train home on Friday. Ida was teary-eyed but understood that her sister was anxious to go home. Papa did not acknowledge that she had spoken; he just asked her to bring him a glass of milk. The girls watched as Papa crumbled his hot cornbread into the cold milk. He added a bit of salt and pepper, stirred the mixture, and ate it with his spoon. Emma had always been intrigued with this concoction. She remembered that it infuriated Matilda when he did this. A little chill ran down Emma's spine as she remembered Matilda screeching at him. *You're getting crumbs on my clean tablecloth!*

Emma crumbled her cornbread into her milk, added the salt and pepper, stirred it, and took a bite. Her nose wrinkled as she swallowed. *What did Papa like about this mess?* She did not think she could finish it but felt she shouldn't waste it. As she sat contemplating the next disgusting bite, Papa reached for her glass. With a little chuckle, he said, "Child, it's an acquired taste, but I'll not ask you to acquire it on my account." Emma laughed, "Papa, I'm not sure I could *ever* acquire a taste for wet sand."

Chapter 5

23 December 1900

Grandpa George and Ida burst through the door like the icy north wind. It was cold enough for snow, and Ida prayed for it every night. Nothing would make the young girl happier than snow at Christmas. Her cheeks flushed from excitement as much as from the cold. Grandpa George had taken her to cut down a Christmas tree. She kept pinching herself, sure she would wake up from this beautiful dream at any moment. Ida was twelve, and in her whole life, she had never had a Christmas tree. Mother would never allow it. She said they were messy, and the house would burn down around their ears if they had

one. Ida had not realized that she desperately wanted a tree until Grandpa
told her they were going to cut one.

When the half-frozen duo returned,
Emma called them to the fireplace to
warm up; she had hot cider, biscuits,
and honey waiting. She loved seeing
her little sister so happy, and Ida's joy
helped ease the melancholy she wal-
lowed in. It would never do for her to
go around like a sad sack and ruin Ida's
fun.

After their refreshments, Grandpa
George brought the tree into the house.
Emma had doubts about whether it
would fit; she had never seen a tree so
large, especially not inside. She didn't
remember Christmas before Momma
died; she had not been much more than
a baby. *Had they had an enormous tree*

when Momma was alive? She would have to ask Lu or Betsy. Grandpa George had nailed boards to the bottom of the trunk, and after considerable effort on all their parts, they managed to get the tree upright. They had to trim a bit here and there, the top bowed over where it touched the ceiling, and the lower limbs reached out to grab as you walked past. Once they finished, they declared it, "The most perfect Christmas tree ever!"

Christmas Eve was even colder than the day before. Emma stirred the fire and set the coffee on to boil. Papa would be awake soon, and she hurried to prepare his breakfast before the family arrived. Emma struggled with her emotions as she did her chores. She was angry when she allowed herself to think about it, which she rarely did.

Papa couldn't help it that he was sick, and Ida was too young to care for him alone. Her brothers and sisters had families, and most lived far away from Liberty Grove. Reminding herself of these things did not ease the sting of disappointment. She was supposed to be back in Caseyville; she was supposed to be helping Charley finish their home; she was supposed to be helping her sisters and Aunt Lucy bake pies and cakes in preparation for *their* Christmas feast.

Emma gave herself a mental shake. She had to stop this brooding. Ida would be up soon, and Emma had promised to help her make paper chains to hang on the tree. Eyeing it, she wondered if they had enough paper. A storm of conflicting emotions raged under her determination to keep her promise to Ida.

Emma carried the tray into Papa's room just as he began to stir from sleep. She made a quick appraisal of his appearance. His color was good; his skin looked healthy again. His thick beard was neatly trimmed, thanks to her nagging. Papa had slept through the night, and she had not heard any coughing or moaning when she checked on him. After helping him sit in a chair, she placed the laptray across his legs and checked his eyes - they looked clear. All these were things to be thankful for, and all these were things that brought her a great deal of frustration. Despite these positive signs, Papa's inability to walk and the mysterious nature of his illness continued to weigh on Emma and the family.

When Papa had been suffering from the poison that Matilda had given him for years, he had always had a faraway, glassy look in his eyes, and he had been muddle-headed and tired. When he had influenza, he had a horrible cough and fever. Papa woke up on the Wednesday after Thanksgiving and called out for her. This sickness, whatever it was, had no visible symptoms except he couldn't walk. Emma had sent for Doctor Perkins and Ma; they had agreed that they could not find anything *wrong* with Papa. Doc said that the arsenic could have damaged his nerves, and his only suggestion was to apply hot compresses and massage Papa's legs several times each day.

Emma had ridden into town and sent Charley another telegram explaining her latest delay, promising to return for

Christmas. It was nearly Christmas; she was still at Papa's, and she had secretly begun wondering if she was supposed to return to Caseyville.

As Emma moved around the room, straightening the bed covers and opening the curtain to let the weak winter sunshine in, Papa sat in his chair, eyes closed. Steam rose from the coffee cup he held and caressed his face.

"Papa, you must eat and keep your strength up. Ida will be up soon, and we'll decorate the tree. Finish your breakfast, then you can sit near the fire and enjoy the festivities." Just when Emma thought he had dozed off, he spoke. "My girl, I do not know how I would ever get along without you. You have always been my rock. After your dear momma passed on, I thought I would go crazy, but there you would be, holding out those little arms, and one more time, I would have the strength to go on. I am so thankful to God that you have returned to stay with me. Ida and I would be plum lost without you." *Stay?* Emma's hands stilled as she smoothed the quilt across the bed. Her heart pounded, and there was a strange roar in her ears. *Stay!*

Surely Papa did not think she meant to *stay*; he *knew* she was returning to Caseyville to marry Charley! Of course, she had come home after the fire; of course, she had stayed then - much longer than she had intended - to care for him and Ida. Papa was injured and sick, then there was rebuilding the house, and… He could not believe that she was going to stay forever! Emma took slow, deep breaths, trying to calm herself before she spoke. She walked to Papa and ran her hand across his forehead, almost hoping he had a fever again and that it was causing him to be confused. His face was cool, and Emma began to panic.

"Papa, I have loved being here with you and Ida. I am very thankful that I have seen you settle in the new house and have been able to help Ida adjust to there being *just the two of you now.* Ida's grown up so much these past months - because she can continue her schooling and will have help from Widow Key and Ma, I can go back to Caseyville with peace in my heart. Knowing that you will be up to taking the train with Ida to visit makes my leaving easier. I know you are anxious to meet the rest of your grandchildren and see all the folks, so I thought that in the Spring…" "Now, girl, stop with that nonsense. It would be much better for us all if the children came here to visit. We can all visit your dear momma at the graveyard, and you and Ida can prepare a feast. I am sure that Ma and the widow would help." Emma felt the shaking start and knew she had to get away from her papa before she began to scream. She picked up the cup he had set aside and mumbled about getting more coffee. Her knees nearly buckled before she made it from the room.

Emma sank to the floor when she stepped from his room. Hot tears streamed down her face as her heart raced. *What was Papa talking about? Why would he think she would be here with Ida to prepare for the visiting folks?* She had to calm herself. Ida was stirring in her room, and Emma could not let her sister find her sitting on the floor crying and shaking like a leaf.

Emma stumbled to the kitchen and stepped outside into the cold, hoping to clear her head. *How had Papa gotten things so mixed up? She needed to talk to Ma. She had her train ticket; she would see Charley within the week. Papa was confused - that was it. He had not meant that she was to stay here; he just meant that she would help Ida when they all visited - all the girls would help.*

Chapter 6

Papa's home was noisy, filled with noisy children and adults. Everyone was talking at once, and Emma was oblivious to everything and everyone around her. Each person spoke to her and asked questions, which she answered. However, she could not recall a single word that she had said. Whatever she said must have been right because no one looked at her like she had lost her mind or had two heads. She tried to concentrate, but she could only focus on Papa talking about her staying here. How would she make him understand that she was leaving in a week?

Emma was aware that Ma was watching her and tried to shake herself free from her distraction. There would be time after dinner to figure out what to do. Now, she needed to focus on her family and the rare treat of spending Christmas with her grandparents. Grandpa George was reading the story of the birth of Jesus from his Bible. He patiently answered the questions from Etta's son, Lee, about how many sheep the shepherds "watched" and whether they brought them to see Baby Jesus. Papa sat near the fire, chatting with Lu's oldest son, Riley. Riley told his grandfather about a mare he had bought and his plans to plant a new field in the spring. Papa's eyes were bright, and his voice was strong as he and Riley discussed the best time to plant and the possibility of Riley breeding his mare to Papa's stud, Copper.

Emma began to feel less anxious about leaving Papa as she watched how he interacted with the family. Lu and Etta were nearby and would look in on him and Ida, as would Grandpa George and Ma. Widow Key and her son would be there to manage the day-to-day chores and would send word if there were any problems. For the first time in weeks, Emma felt like she could breathe and had hope that *this* time, she would make it onto her train back to Caseyville and Charley.

The other women were out in the kitchen finishing the meal they would share at noon. Emma watched Ida move from place to place, wanting to be part of the children gathered near Grandpa George while yearning to be with the women preparing the meal. Emma remembered that feeling of not knowing where she fit in - more woman than a child but not ready to take the last step into adulthood. She would encourage Ida to enjoy her time as a child. Heaven knew she had barely had a chance to be a little girl.

Papa's voice cut through her musings, "Emma, girl, where're you off to? Don't you hear that knocking at the door?" Emma shook her head to clear the musing and hurried to let whoever stood out in the cold inside. Her breath came out in a whoosh when she opened the door and was swept into Charley's arms.

Charley spun her around, allowing him to hold her before setting her back on her feet. Lee had abandoned the story of Jesus's birth to dance around his aunt and the tall, snow-covered man. Emma could not understand a word anyone was saying. Between the pounding of her heart in her ears, the squeals of the children, and the excited voices of the adults, she struggled to make out the words that Charley whispered. "Oh, Emma, I have missed you so. I could not wait another week to see your lovely face. Merry Christmas, my dear one. It's time we go home."

Emma's breathing slowed, and her hearing returned. Ma stood beside her, her arm linked through Charley's, welcoming him to Papa's home. Grandpa George clapped him on the back and said seeing him again was a fine surprise.   Everyone greeted Charley, and the men asked about his horse. Charley explained that he had caught a ride from town with Mr. Hogue, but there *were* parcels out on the porch that he should bring in. As Charley returned through the door with a sack slung over his shoulder, Emma heard Lee gasp, "Santa!"

To Emma, it truly was as if Santa had come. The only way the day could have been better was if the rest of her Caseyville family had been there, too. Everyone gathered around the tables, and after Grandpa George said the blessing over the food, giving special thanks for Charley's presence, they all ate until they could not hold another bite. Emma thought the food was the most delicious she had ever eaten as she gazed at Charley across the table.

When the leftovers had been cleared away, the mystery of what was hidden in their stockings was more than Lee and Ida could stand. As the adults took their time drinking coffee, they watched the children try to sneak peeks at the goodies Santa had left for them; finally, the children began to cause a racket, wanting to see what bounty awaited. Each child exclaimed over the handful of nuts and the shiny apple they received. Their eyes were the size

of saucers as they carefully removed each item and discovered a peppermint stick and a shiny new penny. Under the enormous tree were small packages for the children. Lee was beside himself over the cast iron horse and wagon he discovered, and Ida sat and caressed the lovely brush and comb set she had received.

Emma could not remember a more perfect day. People surrounded her that she loved; she was full of delicious food prepared by loving hands, and Charley sat beside her. Papa smiled and laughed; baby Jim nestled in his arms as he tasted Lee's peppermint stick. All was right with her world.

Emma stepped into the kitchen to check the fire she had banked in the stove. She wanted to ensure the house stayed warm so there wasn't a chance of Papa getting sick again. Charley walked up behind her, settled his hands on her shoulders, and turned her to face him. "Have you any idea how I have missed you? Every day that has passed,

I have fought not to worry that I had only imagined you." Emma placed a hand over one of Charley's and touched her cameo with the other. Yes, all was truly right with her world. Charley was not only real, but he had missed her, and in a few days, they would be leaving for Caseyville to start their life together.

Charley took the hand that rested on his and turned it so that he could place a small box in her palm. Emma's hands trembled as she pressed the tiny latch; the lid popped open to reveal a delicate locket suspended from a gold ribbon-shaped pin. Emma carefully removed it from the box and opened the case, following Charley's instructions, to reveal a tiny image of his face. "I hope it's not too presumptuous to think you would want a likeness of me. I often wished for one of you while we have been apart." Emma's eyes brimmed with tears as she fastened the delicate pin to the bodice of her dress. "Oh, Charley, now you'll always be near my heart!"

As the day wore on, they made plans to have a farewell supper with the family before they took the train back to Caseyville on Friday. With only two days left at her Papa's, Emma listed everything she needed to do before they left. It wasn't easy to focus on her task when she started thinking she would welcome the new year with her Caseyville family and Charley.

Chapter 7

As the train engine built up steam, the smoke billowing from the stack looked like snow clouds in the crisp morning air. Emma and Charley had said goodbyes the evening before. It was too cold for the family to wait at the train depot with them. Emma recalled the past few days as they huddled near the wood stove.

Everyone had promised to keep a close eye on Papa and ensure Ida did not fall behind in school or become overwhelmed by her new responsibilities as "lady of the house." Widow Key assured Emma that if she noticed any decline in Papa's health, she would send for Ma and Doc Perkins *and* send

Emma a telegram, then hugged her tightly and told her, "Don't you be worrying yourself, get busy building a life with your young man!" Ma and Grandpa George had promised her that they would look after Ida especially. Emma hated leaving her grandparents; she had just gotten to know them and now didn't know when she would see them again.

She and Ida had shared Ida's room since Charley had arrived on Christmas, Emma treasuring every moment with her little sister. She thought about her final conversation with Ida: "Ida, darling, you must promise me to keep up with your schoolwork and that you will go for Ma or one of the girls if you need help. I know you and Papa will be fine, but I can't help but worry about both of you. You must promise to write to me every week and tell me about your friends, church, Papa, and *everything*! And Ida, please, don't ever hide your beautiful voice again. You bring such joy to others with your songs."

Then there was Papa… he was in good spirits; his appetite was hearty, he rarely coughed, and his eyes were clear. When she told the family she was going back to Caseyville with Charley, Papa did not object. Emma had almost convinced herself that she had overreacted to what Papa had said about her remaining in Liberty Grove. Something still nagged at her, though. She wouldn't call it worry, exactly, more of an uneasiness. Papa had been through so much in the past few months, and Emma could not bear it if something were to happen to him now. She comforted herself that he was in capable hands and seemed excited for her when he had told her goodbye this morning. He had even gotten up from his chair to clap Charley on the back and tell him, "Take good care of our girl."

The engineer blew the whistle, and they climbed aboard, excited to be headed toward the new life they would soon make together. As the train swayed down the tracks, Emma was lulled into a peacefulness she had not felt since the night Charley had asked her to marry him.

Emma was surprised when Charley gently shook her awake. The last time she had ridden a train was when she returned to Liberty Grove after the fire. It was funny how each trip she had made was so drastically different. Her first trip to Caseyville was a mixture of terror of the unknown, the excitement of the train's speed, and, of course, seeing her sisters. The trip after the fire was the longest eight hours of her life. She had felt she could get home faster by walking, and her brother, Albert, had even threatened to tie her to her seat because she was so agitated. With Charley seated next to her on this trip, she truly felt she was going home. She realized that she had been under a great deal of strain the past few months, and having Charley near, she had felt safe and relaxed enough to sleep much of the way.

As they neared the station, they talked about when they first met that summer and everything that had changed. They planned to stay at Uncle Frank's and Aunt Lucy's since it was so cold and late. Charley would take her to Betsy's in the morning after they had driven out to see the progress on their new home. Charley had described the house and barn vividly, but Emma was anxious to see everything herself. She would have loved to see Betsy tonight, but it was too cold to risk the trip. She would have to wait until tomorrow to see her sisters and their families.

The train eased into the station, and Emma was out of her seat before it stopped. She had not realized just how excited she was to be home. Papa's house was, well, Papa's, but here, with Charley, this was truly her home. She was so lost in this new realization that she walked straight into Betsy's arms without seeing her standing there.

"Betsy, oh Betsy, I have missed you so much! I didn't think I would see you until tomorrow. What a wonderful surprise!" The sisters hugged, laughed, and talked over each other until finally, Doc stepped in and said, "Ladies, let's get you over to Ma and Pa's before those tears of joy turn to icicles." Charley had loaded their bags into the wagon, and after wrapping thick blankets around the women's shoulders and legs, they set off on the short but cold trip.

Emma was shocked when they got inside, and Agnes, Maggie, Sallie, and their families were there. The smell of delicious food and strong, hot coffee filled the air as everyone passed Emma around for hugs and talked at once. She could not help but think about how much this was like the day she first came to Caseyville – she had come here a young, scared girl uncertain of her future and now returned a confident, engaged woman.

Chapter 8

Emma and her sisters sat up until the early morning hours. The children had been put to bed on pallets covering Aunt Lucy's parlor floor. The men had hunkered down in the barn, insisting that the hay would keep them warm and that they were tough enough to manage a night of "roughing it." Uncle Frank had wished them luck as he headed off to his warm, soft bed with Aunt Lucy.

Emma's sisters caught her up on all the local news, filling in details left out of their letters. The biggest news was that Grace Webb and Ed Simmons had broken off their engagement. Ed had moved off to Oklahoma Territory, having gotten wind of the fact that there might be another land lottery in the new year. Grace had been heartbroken for a while, but Clem Kincaid had taken notice of her, and she had perked up a bit.

In time, the talk turned to Papa and the folks back in Liberty Grove. It felt good to be able to unburden herself to her sisters. After discussing all of Papa's setbacks and the tragedy of the fire, they moved on to Ida and the renewed relationship with Ma and Grandpa George. Talking with her sisters, Emma felt peace about leaving Papa and Ida alone.

No matter how she begged or tried to turn the conversation around, her sisters refused to discuss the one thing she wanted most to talk about: her new house. They all agreed that Charley had the right to show her their home without them spoiling his surprise.

When the clock struck 3 a.m., they decided they best try to sleep; the men would be up to do chores for Uncle Frank soon before they headed home to tend their livestock. As Betsy and Emma lay under the quilt in their shared bed, Betsy whispered, "I am so glad that Charley went to get you. We were all worried that you had decided not to come back home. Charley was beside himself, thinking you had changed your mind about wanting to marry him. One day, Agnes stamped her foot and said, "If you want her back here, you had best go and get her!" Charley bought a ticket that day, and well, here we all are."

In the morning, the men did not want to admit how cold it was in the barn. The amount of steaming coffee they drank and the good-natured jostling for a place closest to the fire told the true tale. Those who had spent a warm night inside did not doubt the kind of adventure it had *really* been. After a hot and hearty breakfast, everyone bundled into their wagons and headed home. Emma and Charley stayed behind to help clean up and put the house in order. When everything was put away, and Charley had checked on the livestock and brought more wood in for the third time, Aunt Lucy picked up her spoon and said, "Boy, if you don't take this girl to see her new house, I'm going to have to take this spoon to your backside." Laughing, Charley kissed her wrinkled cheek and told Emma to hurry and save him from Aunt Lucy's wrath.

The ride to the farm was cold but pleasant. Emma wondered if her excitement kept her from freezing. Charley gave the horses their heads, and they wasted no time making their way to the barn, where sweet hay and shelter from the wind awaited.

As they pulled up on the ridge overlooking Jim and Maggie's pond, the house came into sight, and Emma's mouth formed that perfect little "O" that Charley found so charming. It was rare that she was speechless, but no matter how she tried, she could not find words to express what she was feeling the moment she saw the house that Charley had built for them to share.

It was *perfect*. A deep porch looked out over the pond. Emma could see them sitting there in the evening, watching the sunset and their children playing  in the grass... Emma's cheeks flamed. For the first time since Charley brought her to this spot and asked her to marry him, she realized that the man sitting next to her would be her husband, that they would one day, by the grace of God, have children and grow old together like Ma and Grandpa George. For the first time, she realized how deeply she loved Charley and wanted to spend the rest of her life with him. "Thank you. Thank you for coming to get me. Thank you for not giving up when I was delayed over and over.

Thank you for believing in our future and building this beautiful home."

"Emma, would you like to go inside?" Charley helped her down from the wagon and held his breath as she stepped inside their home for the first time. "Emma, anything you do not like, we can change. I asked your sisters about things, but this is *your* house, and I want you to have it just how you want it." Emma turned a slow circle as she took in the craftsmanship. There was a large stone fireplace in the kitchen, big enough that she could boil a pot of water for laundry in the winter or cook a pot of stew large enough to feed all their family. A shiny new wood stove with two warming ovens stood on another wall. She noticed a cabinet under a window with a pump for water. Tears began to run down her cheeks as she looked at all the thoughtful touches Charley had added to their home. She only prayed that she would be worthy of everything he had done for her. Charley noticed her tears and began to panic. *She hated it, she was disappointed. If she would give him a chance, he would fix it.*

"Emma, please don't cry! I can change whatever it is you don't like." "Oh, Charley, I love everything about it; why would you change a thing?" Charley pulled her into his arms and breathed his first easy breath since the day she had agreed to marry him. He had not realized how anxious he'd been about the house and her being away for so long. It had been hard not to lose hope when the days had turned into weeks and months. He had not wanted to pressure her; he knew her papa needed her, but he was sure thankful she was with him now.

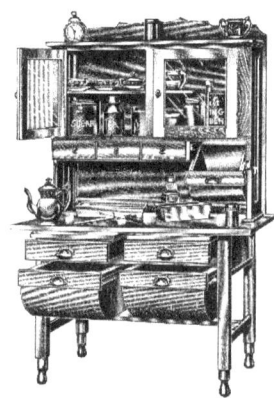

They walked through the house, looking at every detail and dreaming about their life together. Behind the kitchen was a shed room where Emma could store canned goods and other staples. There was the most delightful cabinet in that room. Charley called it a Hoosier Cabinet. It had a flour bin and glass storage jars, room to store spices, and a cutting board. Emma was already thinking of asking Charley to move it into the kitchen as she planned to use it daily. A wide dogtrot separated the kitchen from the living area. Charley had fitted the open ends with heavy doors for the winter. In the milder weather, they would open the doors to help cool the house in the Texas heat. In the living area was another fireplace, a twin to the one in the kitchen. Emma could imagine sitting near the fire on cool nights, knitting or mending, and listening to Charley read from the Bible. Behind the parlor were two smaller rooms; one would be their bedroom, and eventually, the second would be the children's room. Charley explained that the way he had designed the house, a stairway in the dogtrot led to the attic, and one day, when their children were older, he would add more bedrooms up there. Emma's cheeks turned bright pink again at the thought of that.

After walking through the house and admiring everything again, Emma began to wish for paper and a pencil. She wanted to make notes about curtains and what she would need for each room. She had a few items she had made and put away for when she eventually married, but now she needed to get serious. She was anxious to talk to her sisters; they would all be excited to help her sew curtains and quilts for her new home. In the back of her mind, she added soft wool yarn to her list, a light green, for a baby blanket. She would tuck it away for someday...

Chapter 9

1901 –

Emma wrote weekly to Ida, Papa, Ma, and Grandpa George. In her letters, she painted a vivid picture of the house that Charley had built and of the farm where they would live. She wanted to share as much of her new life as possible with them.

She was excited to be close enough to Maggie to walk to her house whenever she wanted. When she noticed that her kitchen window overlooked the pond where she had chucked a rock at Charley, he teased her that there had never been another choice for where to put their house. It was not often that Emma's temper got the better of her, but that one time… Charley would see her gazing out the window, grin, and rub his cheek. Sometimes, you must endure a bit of pain to reap the best reward.

At least once a week, Charley took Emma to see the progress of the house. Seeing it change from a shell to a home was a miracle to her. They bought two comfortable chairs and spent hours deciding where to place them in the parlor. Charley and Jim built a dining table, and Doc and Amos helped Charley build the chairs and benches. The day she hung the curtains she had made in her kitchen window, Emma wept with happiness. The sun slanting through the window made a slash of warmth across the floor. Emma could envision an orange tabby cat napping there.

The letters Emma received from Ida brought her joy. She and Papa had settled into an easy routine. Her schoolwork was going well, and she was keeping her grades up. Papa let her have friends over, and she was proud of her beautiful room. Emma was thrilled that her little sister was finally enjoying her life. Ida wrote that for Easter, she had been asked to sing a special song at church, *Christ the Lord Is Risen Today.* She was a little nervous, but Ma kept reminding her that God had given her a beautiful voice, and she should use it for His glory.

Ma wrote to Emma as well. She and Grandpa George were doing "fine as frog's hair." They looked forward to warmer weather; the cold was hard on their rheumatism. She confirmed that Papa and Ida were doing well and that they were all hoping to visit in the Summer. Ma told Emma she had something special for her new house and would bring it when they came.

Overall, life was good. Charley had made their first crop. They had a sturdy barn and a cozy home. Emma had planted roses, and Betsy was helping her lay out a spring garden. They had a good well, and Charley and Jim were fiddling with ways to make it easier to water the plants if they didn't get rain when needed.

Being near her sisters, brothers, and their families was exactly what Emma needed - she watched how they worked together as partners, the women providing an attractive and comfortable home for the hard-working men and how the men showed their appreciation for a well-cooked meal and a restful place at the end of a long day. Emma hid her observations in her heart and promised that she would be a helper to Charley, now and when she was his wife.

Emma realized that the home she had grown up in had been far removed from her siblings' loving, nurturing homes. She thought about Ma and Grandpa George about Aunt Lucy and Uncle Frank, how they worked together and loved each other, and she wondered if her momma and papa had been like that with each other. Matilda had never provided a cozy home, and Emma had always felt on edge. She vowed that her children would always feel loved and secure.

They had decided on a summer wedding. Emma would be seventeen in March. It would be easier for her Liberty Grove Family to attend in the summer. Ida would be out of school, and finding someone to look after the stock would not be a problem. With a tentative plan for June, Betsy, Maggie, Agnes, and Sallie began to plan and sew in earnest.

The winter slowly loosened its grip, and Emma noticed that tiny bits of green were poking their way out of the ground. The new life made her heart sing as she looked ahead to the life she would soon start with Charley. One evening, late in March, Betsy surprised her by saying she had invited the entire family to come out on Saturday after Emma's birthday. They planned a day of food and celebration, and Betsy informed Emma that she was to do nothing but enjoy being the guest of honor. Charley had already asked her to have supper with him on her birthday, and honestly, she was feeling very spoiled by all the attention.

When Emma opened her eyes on Friday, March 29, 1901, she lay in bed thinking about how drastically her life had changed. Last year, Papa had sent her to stay with Betsy. She had worried herself sick over leaving Papa and what might happen to him if she were not there to look out for him. As it turned out, horrible things did happen, but more good than bad had come from it. The best thing that happened was Charley. Emma could scarcely believe that it had been nearly a year since she met the tall man with the beautiful blue eyes who had captured her heart and would soon be her husband. Emma giggled as she rose from her bed. *Who would have thought throwing a rock at someone could lead to marriage?* Her eyes widened as she spied what Betsy had draped across the chair during the night.

Emma did not think there could ever be a dress prettier than the one Betsy had made for her last birthday, but this one was beautiful *and* grown up. Betsy had chosen cream-colored linen, and Emma was certain that the pale blue, fancy stitching on the fitted sleeves and bodice was Sallie's handiwork. As she examined it more closely, she discovered signs of Agnes, Maggie, and Aunt Lucy's needlework. Tears welled in her eyes and overflowed just as Betsy knocked on her door and entered the room. "Oh, Emma, is something wrong with your dress?" Emma held the dress at arm's length, not wanting to spoil it with her tears, and continued to cry. "Honey, whatever it is, we can fix it. I'll get the girls together, and it will be perfect before you know it." Emma shook her head and whispered, "Betsy, it *is* perfect; it is the most beautiful dress in the world. I'm crying because my heart is bursting from all the love that went into making it for me."

When Emma went down for breakfast, she had another surprise. Her oldest brother, Albert, was sitting at the table drinking coffee from his saucer. Emma watched as he blew across the steaming liquid and then inhaled it. She had seen Grandpa George do the same thing, which always fascinated her.

Albert wrapped her in one of his bear hugs, kissed the top of her head, and said, "Happy Birthday, baby sister." It was because of Albert that she had met Charley. When Emma visited last year, Betsy encouraged her to make a box lunch for the social at church. Emma was shy, did not know anyone, and was embarrassed that no one would bid on her lunch, so Betsy had arranged for Albert to bid on Emma's dinner, *and* he stayed in the bidding up to $8.00, an unheard-of amount. Then, Charley called out, *"I bid twenty dollars!"* Albert dropped out of the bidding and left his baby sister with a flaming red face and the beginning of a romance.

"I brought you a present, my girl. With all the sewing and such you ladies have been doin', Ma thought you might need a place to keep your treasures. Her papa made it for her when she was younger than you. I had co-op business down their way, and she asked me to bring it back to you." For the second time that morning, Emma's eyes flooded with tears. What a glorious day this was turning out to be! She had a beautiful new dress that her beloved sisters and aunt had sewn just for her, and now she had her grandmother's hope chest. Emma could not wait to fill it with the pretty things for her new home.

Emma ran her hands lovingly over the carvings, a testament to her great-grandfather's love for his daughter. How odd that a man she had never met had built this more than sixty years ago, yet she could feel the love he had put into it, even today. She opened the lid to find even more surprises. Inside was a small package from Papa and Ida, a strand of blue beads; Ida had embroidered a soft pouch for Emma to keep them in. Ma had sent a set of fancy embroidered tea towels as if the chest were not present enough. This was, without a doubt, the best birthday Emma had ever had!

After breakfast, Betsy shooed her out of the kitchen with orders to enjoy her special day. Emma would not have minded helping Betsy with the dishes and preparations for tomorrow's party, but Betsy knew that growing up, Emma never had a special birthday. She had been so young when their Momma died, and Papa married Matilda. Once Matilda joined the family, there were no celebrations. Betsy wanted her little sister to have a day that was all about her and what she wanted to do.

Albert carried Ma's - well, her - hope chest up to her room, and Emma began to sort through the things she had sewn for her and Charley's home. Emma knew that she could take them to the house, but she found herself wanting to touch them, often, as if that made her coming wedding real. After she had sorted and admired each piece and decided what to put into the chest and what she wanted to work on just a bit more, she sat down to write letters to Ma and the rest of her family in Liberty Grove.

Emma thanked Ma for the chest and the lovely towels. She wrote about her new dress and described in detail the special touches that each woman had added. She wrote to Ida and complimented her on the embroidery she had done on the bead pouch. She missed her little sister and looked forward to seeing her in the summer. She told Ida how she wished she could hear her sing at Easter and reminded her that her voice was as beautiful as an angel's and there was no reason for her to be nervous.

When she wrote to Papa, she thanked him for the beads, telling him that she recognized them from Momma's likeness and how special it was that he had given them to her. Each bead was painted with a tiny flower in a softer shade of blue. Emma had spent hours studying Momma's likeness when it was hidden away in the attic. Papa had always said that Emma reminded him of Jane and had often mistaken her for her momma when he was ill. Knowing that Papa had given them to Jane when they married and passed them on to her made Emma's heart soar. Looking at all the lovely items she had received that day, she felt Momma and Ma were beside her and thought, *how could this day get any better?*

Chapter 10

Charley knocked on the door at precisely 5 p.m. He was as nervous as he had been the first time he had called for Emma. While he hadn't driven up and down the road until it was time to knock, this time, he had sat in his buggy, staring at his watch until it was time to pick Emma up. He did not know why he felt he had to be so precise, but he did. Doc met him at the door, the thought crossing his mind that the more things changed, the more they stayed the same. Charley's hair was slicked down so tight to his scalp it looked like it would hurt, and once again, he held flowers, only this time they had not been hastily picked from Betsy's garden.

Doc led him into the kitchen, offered coffee, saw how Charley's hands shook and thought better of that. Betsy would skin him if Emma's beau were stained or burned when she came down, so he set a glass of water in front of the young man. Charley downed the entire glass, let the breath he had held out in a rush, and sank into a chair. *Why was he so all-fired nervous?* As he began to breathe again, he heard Betsy call from the front room that Emma was ready.

Charley had never seen anything as lovely as Emma. She wore her new dress, and the cameo he had given her for last year's birthday was pinned to a blue ribbon on her bodice. She wore a strand of cobalt glass beads that picked up the faint color of the flowers stitched into her dress. Charley felt his heart would burst. *How had he ever won the love of this beautiful girl?*

Betsy smiled as she watched the blush spread across her younger sister's cheeks, and Charley stared at Emma as if dumbfounded. Betsy thought of her momma then and hoped she could somehow see her baby girl and the man so obviously smitten with her. One of the last things Momma had said to her was, "See to Emma; make sure she's happy and loved." Well, it had taken a while, and the road had not been easy, but there was no doubt that Emma was both happy and loved. "Charley, how about I put those flowers in water so you and Emma can be on your way?" When Charley did not surrender the flowers, Betsy gently took them from

his hand as Doc turned the young couple toward the door and their destiny.
As he closed the door and turned to his
wife, Doc chortled, "I've never seen
two folks that were quite so moon-eyed
as those two."

Charley helped Emma step into the
buggy and tried to clear his muddled
thoughts as he climbed up on the other
side. Only after he had settled in next
to her did he realize he had forgotten to
untie his horse, Old Jumper. When they
had met last summer, Emma had as-
sumed he was simple-minded; Charley
wondered if she was right! He certainly
could not keep his thoughts straight tonight. Charley had not believed she
could be lovelier than she had been the
day she had thrown that rock at him. He
rubbed his cheek as he remembered
how the little blonde streaks in her dark

hair reminded him of sunlight and how she was crying or mad every time they were together. She might send him packing or hurl another rock his way if he didn't get his head out of the clouds.

As Charley climbed back into the buggy, he realized they had not spoken. His voice cracked slightly as he said, "That's a right pretty dress, and those beads are lovely." Emma blushed, and a satisfied smile crept into her eyes. She knew she should not be vain, but it did please her that Charley found her attractive. Her words came out in a rush. "Thank you, Charley. The dress was a gift from my sisters and Aunt Lucy. Each of them added their special touch with the fancy stitches. Papa sent the beads to me; they belonged to my momma. Ma had Albert bring me the hope chest her papa made for her!"

"Well, now, you have had a right special day. I have a little something for you, as well. We might drive to our farm if you're not too hungry." Emma nodded and sat back to enjoy the ride. She loved their farm and could not wait until they were married, and she could spend every day there. As she went about her chores and helped Betsy around her home, Emma would dream about where she would put their furniture in each room and how the curtains she had made would look fluttering in a soft breeze. She would imagine the roses she had planted, covered in blooms, and sitting on the porch with Charley, looking out over the pond. Emma was restless, ready to begin this new chapter in her life. She was so caught up in her daydream that she did not realize they had arrived at the farm and that Charley was patiently holding his hand out to help her step down from the buggy.

Charley continued to hold Emma's hand as they walked toward the house. She thought how nice it felt to have her small hand tucked into his larger work-worn one. Being with Charley made her feel protected and incredibly special.

Charley paused as they reached the door and turned to her, placing his hands gently on each side of her up-turned face. "Happy Birthday, Emma. I bought you a little something for our new home. Now, if it is not to your liking, you say so, and we'll get you something different. Mrs. Driver, at the mercantile, said she had seen you admire it." Charley opened the door and turned her to face the softly lit room. Emma's

hands flew to her mouth, covering that perfect little "O" that her lips formed, but not before Charley saw it and smiled. The chairs they had arranged before the fireplace now flanked a small table. Sitting on the table was the most beautiful lamp Emma had ever seen. She *had* admired it in the mercantile on one of her trips with Betsy but had never dreamed it could be hers; it was so costly. Emma had told herself that a plain oil lamp gave out the same light as a fancy one and pushed it from her mind. It was beautiful, and the light was soft through the painted globe. What a wonder it was, but she had to tell Charley he must return it. They could buy a house full of plain lamps for the price of this one!

Charley watched the emotions play across Emma's face – from surprise to delight to dismay. "Emma, dear, what's wrong? We can return it, and you can pick something you would like." "Oh, Charley, no. I love it; it's the most beautiful thing ever. It's just that it's so costly, and Charley, you've spent so much on our beautiful home already. I can't let you waste your hard-earned money on something so fanciful." "Emma, haven't you figured out by now that making you happy brings me great joy? I know you don't need fancy things, but I'd like to give them to you as long as possible. Our life may be hard at times, but hopefully, when times are tough, the treasures you have will bring you a smile and help you through. I know the Good Book tells us not to put our stock in earthly things, but I think the Lord doesn't much mind us having something nice to look at. So, if that little lamp suits you, then Happy Birthday; if not, we'll find something else that will."

To neither of their surprise, Emma began to cry. Through tears of joy, she reached out to lovingly caress the intricate brasswork of the lamp and then closed her eyes as she stored away the memory of this perfect birthday so she could bring it out on days that weren't so happy and be reminded of all the people that she was blessed to love and be loved by.

Chapter 11

Saturday dawned with a hint of rain in the air. Emma knew her family well enough to know that a bit of bad weather would not stop them from celebrating her birthday. Betsy and Maggie were a force to be reckoned with when they set their minds to something, and the safest thing a body could do was follow their command or get far, far out of their way.

Doc had suggested they could set up tables in the barn if it rained, but Betsy stopped that notion. With all the family there, that meant extra horses in the barn, and she was not inclined to have the aroma of manure wafting through the air while they ate. She planned to push all the parlor furniture against the walls and set up tables inside and on the porch. They might not all be at the same table, but they would be dry, and Sallie suggested that when it was time for cake, they could all switch places. That way, everyone would get to talk with Emma.

Each time Emma tried to help, someone shooed her away. "This is your special day, no work for you!" or "Don't be a silly goose; the birthday girl is supposed to relax." Finally, she wandered out to Betsy's garden. They might not let her help with anything else, but at least she could pick flowers for the tables. That was where Charley found her, arms overflowing with irises, flags his ma had called them. Charley watched as she moved from bloom to bloom, searching for the perfect ones before deftly cutting the stem with a little knife and adding the stalk to her burden.

In a few weeks, it would be a year since he had met her, and shortly after that, they would be married. He remembered Aunt Lucy saying that the older a body got, the faster the time went. In some ways, it was exactly how he felt; in others, he did not think that June would ever get here. Charley knew it was silly but could not help worrying that something else would happen to keep them apart. He wanted, more than anything, to marry Emma and be able to provide for her and protect her. He knew what her life had been like before she had come to live with her sister, Betsy. Albert had told him how poorly their stepmother had treated Emma. Charley just wanted her to be safe and happy. He wanted to be the one who sheltered her from the world and anything in it that might hurt or upset her.

Dinner was loud and joyful. When a large family got together, there was much to say, and everyone talked at once. Emma smiled as she listened to talk of crops to be planted and stock to be tended, cleaning and canning to be done, and the latest news of their neighbors. A sense of happiness came over her as she looked around at the beloved faces of her family. While she was growing up, there had never been meals such as this. Matilda would not allow them, and Emma had certainly never had a day when she was expected to do nothing but enjoy herself.

Mealtime at home with Papa had been quiet. There had been no sharing of the day's events, not even talking about the weather. Once more, it struck Emma how much she and Ida had missed. Emma determined that if she and Charley were someday blessed with children, they would grow up creating memories of large family gatherings where everyone talked at once. Where the children were not only seen but encouraged to join in the conversation. The singing of *Happy Birthday to You* brought her back to the present.

Betsy had baked the most beautiful coconut cake. Emma hated to spoil it by cutting the first slice, but the thought of how delicious it would taste won out as she began to serve her family. Charley glanced around to ensure everyone had been served and asked if he might have a second slice, declaring it "the tastiest thing he had ever eaten." Emma made a mental note to ask Betsy for the recipe. As she took a bite, she decided that Charley was right; it *was* tasty, and this *was* the best birthday that she had ever had.

Chapter 12

A cold spell at Easter worried them about their crops and gardens, but once the sun reappeared, the plants seemed to double in size. Emma helped with the chores at Betsy's, and all the women got together to can the vegetables they picked from their gardens. Emma checked her little garden as often as possible and was pleased to find her plants growing well. She was anxious for the day when she would be there every day to tend her vegetables and her roses.

The wedding plans were almost done. They had decided to get married on June 15th. Papa, Ida, Ma, Grandpa George, and even Luella, Jessie, and

Etta's families planned to come the day before. Emma was excited about having so many of her family surrounding her on their special day. She had insisted that she wear her birthday dress, but Betsy and Maggie would not hear of it. She must have a dress as special as she was, something made just for that day. Her oldest sister, Lu, had sent a cream-colored lace that she had bought on a trip to Austin; Jessie had included the palest blue silk thread in the package, saying that she was sure that one of her sisters could find a clever way to use it in sewing Emma's dress. Even Ida had sent something. She had heard about the tradition of a bride having something old, something new, something borrowed, something blue, and a lucky sixpence for their shoe. Emma's dress would be new, and something blue would be the blue thread; Ma was taking something old when they went to the wedding. That left borrowed and a sixpence, whatever that was. Ida could not think of anything for Emma to borrow, but her teacher told her that a sixpence was like a penny. Mrs. Eason, at the mercantile, let Ida help her after school, and Ida sent one of the shiny pennies she had earned for Emma to wear in her in one of her shoes. Ida hoped it brought her sister luck and not a sore foot.

Emma's hope chest was full, and each time she and Charley visited their farm, the house looked more like a home. A colorful rag rug lay on the floor before the fire in the parlor. Emma had moved the chairs a dozen times and likely would move them a dozen more times, trying to find the perfect spot. Each time she visited, she would lovingly caress the lamp Charley had given her and dream about the time, not too far away, when they would sit together in that very room.

Charley had moved the Hoosier cabinet into her kitchen. A cast iron pot was hanging from a hook in the fireplace. The crisp white curtains she had sewn fluttered in the breeze from the window. Charley laughed when he realized that she had embroidered a row of little fish along the hem, a reminder of when Charley had tried to teach her to fish at the pond below.

In the shed room behind the kitchen, Charley had built shelves, and they were quickly filling up as her sisters insisted that she take part in the bounty each time they canned. Charley had begun to live at the house instead of staying with Aunt Lucy and Uncle Frank.

He had his stock in the barn and had built Emma a chicken coop. Since he no longer lived with his aunt and uncle, he and the other men took turns helping with Uncle Frank's chores, and Aunt Lucy enjoyed seeing "all of her boys" more often.

One day, when Charley was at his aunt and uncle's, Emma stopped in; a small crate was sitting on the table in Aunt Lucy's kitchen. The two ladies sat at the table drinking cold milk, eating hot biscuits, and laughing about how Aunt Lucy always had to swat Charley with her spoon for trying to sneak a biscuit before it was time to eat. Aunt Lucy told Emma what a blessing Charley had been when he came to live with them after his parents and sister had died. She told Emma that Charley was like her own son and that she was so thankful that God had brought Emma to him for a wife. "Emma, open that little box; your Uncle Frank loosened the lid for you." Emma did as Aunt Lucy told her; the most beautiful cruet set was inside the box, carefully packed in straw. "That belonged to Charley's momma, Clara; only a handful of her things made the trip from East Texas to

here after she passed. This was her favorite; I've kept it packed away all these years. I think the time for it to be used and loved again has come." Emma's eyes brimmed with tears, and she could see the silver holder sitting on her kitchen table, sunlight winking off the cut glass cruet bottles. What a special addition to their home, like having Charley's ma with them. "Oh, Aunt Lucy, how can I ever thank you! It *is* the most beautiful thing I have ever seen." *Maybe, if it wasn't too late when Charley finished the chores, they could drive out to the farm, and she could see it sitting on the table for real.*

Chapter 13

12 June 1901 –

Charley and Emma had spent the day at the farm. All of Emma's belongings had been moved to the new house. Ma's hope chest was at the foot of the bed in their room. A new washstand with a flowered bowl and pitcher sat in one corner, and a rocker sat near the wood stove. Emma had never dreamed of such luxury, but Charley insisted that he

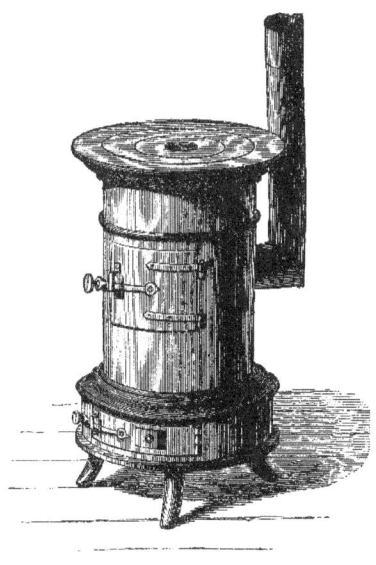

had spent plenty enough cold nights to last a lifetime, and if he had his way about it, he would not spend another one. Emma thought their room looked as cozy as anything she had ever seen. A thick rug covered the floor, and the ladies at church had sewn a charming quilt for them, which was folded across the bed.

Emma had rearranged the parlor furniture again, and Charley had added a little padded stool in front of her chair. The crockery they had purchased was on a shelf in the kitchen. Wood had been brought in for both fireplaces. They would not need a fire for some time yet, but it looked homey, having it stacked nearby. Clara's cruet set was in a place of honor on the table. Emma's brother, Amos, had built a swing and hung it on the front porch, and brightly colored pillows invited a body to settle in and enjoy the view of the pond they shared with Jim and Maggie.

Tomorrow, they would all meet the train and have supper in town. Albert had insisted that the ladies had enough to do on Saturday without spending the day cooking and cleaning up after the hoard that would descend upon them. Supper for the entire family at the cafe would be his contribution to the wedding.

At noon, Charley was looking for a cow that had wandered off. Maggie had sent her daughter, Ada, to the house with a dinner basket. Emma was too hungry to wait on Charley and took one of the sandwiches Maggie had made out to the swing. She was shocked when she stepped onto the porch and saw a strange man standing on the steps.

"May I help you, sir?" Emma heard the tremor in her voice and tried to steady it. She didn't recognize the man, but that did not mean she should be afraid. "Is your man around?" Emma could not shake the feeling of uneasiness as she took in the man's scraggly beard and noticed a faded green patch on his coat sleeve. She took a deep breath before speaking. "Well, my *husband* is just there, umm, beyond the tree line, bringing in a cow that got loose. I will be happy to fetch him for you." She hoped he didn't notice her slight hesitation about Charley's location. "No, ma'am, I'll just wait a bit for him." Rising panic kept her from thinking clearly. There was no reason to fear this man, but something didn't feel right to her. If Charley hurried and came home, or if she could get inside the house, she would be fine. She stepped back toward the door, but the man moved slightly closer. Now, a prickle of fear ran up her spine. She needed to put space between them. "Sir, you look hot and dusty. The well water is cool, and there's a dipper hanging right by the bucket. You're welcome to help your-

self." Emma said a little prayer that the man would accept her offer. After hesitating, he turned and walked to the well. Emma waited for only a moment before slipping into the house. As soon as the door closed, she leaned against it, trying to think what to push in front of it to keep him out. She wished that Charley had put a latch on it. If she had a latch, she could breathe again. She thought about running out the back door and trying to get to Maggie's, but what if Charley returned and she wasn't there to warn him about the man? What if the man was there to harm him?

Emma shook herself and managed to slow her pounding heart. She needed to watch the man and listen for Charley. She decided the best thing to do was watch him from the kitchen window, As she walked past the heavy cabinet, that she desperately wished she was strong enough to move, she picked up her rolling pin. If he tried to come inside, she would do her best to brain him with it and throw whatever she could find at him. She was pretty good at hitting her target with a rock!

Emma eased the curtain back and looked toward the well. The man wasn't there! She tried to see where he might be hiding but couldn't see the whole yard from her vantage point. Sweat trickled down her neck as she realized he might be climbing through one of the windows she had opened earlier. What if he'd gone looking for Charley, or what if he'd gone towards Maggie's? Was she there alone with the children? Emma had to move; she said a prayer, asking God to give her courage and protection, and with her rolling pin gripped tightly, she headed into battle.

Emma eased the door open, half expecting him to jump out at her, and flinched when he didn't. After scanning the yard and out by the well, she stepped outside. She inched her way off the porch and along the side of the house. Emma didn't see him out by the barn or chicken coop; truth be told, she was too frightened to look inside, so she would try to keep them in her sight until Charley came home. The sun had warmed the walls of the house, and the heat against her back gave her courage. She had just turned the corner to return to the well when she heard a cow's bell and realized Charley was nearby. She had to warn him about the stranger; she couldn't let the man ambush him. Should she yell for him, or maybe if she could find a rock, she could get his attention that way. Emma spied a rock and was poised to let it fly in Charley's direction when she heard Maggie yelling, "Emma! Emma!"

Fear left her as she rushed to her sister's aid; terror gave way to rage.

Maggie and Charley saw her at the same time. Not realizing that she thought they were in danger and was there to protect them, they saw a diminutive warrior, rolling pin in one hand, rock in the other, charging straight toward the strange man. Charley reached her before she struck her first blow but caught a sharp heel to his shin for his trouble. "Emma, Emma! It's all right; I'm here. You're safe." Adrenaline rushed through her veins; her heart pounded in her ears. *Why was Charley restraining **her** and not the man?* Maggie and Charley were talking, and the man was talking, but she couldn't understand what they were saying. Maggie pushed a dipper of cool water into her hands and encouraged her to drink while Charley continued restraining her.

The whooshing sound in her ears had quieted. If she understood correctly, Mrs. Eason had sent the man with a message for Charley. When Emma had acted so strangely and run into the house, he'd gone to fetch someone, thinking she was ill, and met Maggie on the path.

Emma's cheeks flamed in embarrassment as she realized that she had been about to knock the man on the head with her rolling pin; then she grew angry that he hadn't simply told her why he was there and saved her from getting so worked up. The rock was still gripped in her hand, and the thought that she could still give him a little bonk on his noggin' made her feel some better. The man was talking again, and Maggie's gasp brought her out of her reverie. What were they saying?   Her ears started pounding again, and her world went black when her mind grasped the words, "Papa had suffered an apoplexy."

Chapter 14

It had been a little over two weeks since Emma returned to Liberty Grove. Once she had come around, Charley had read the telegram to her about Papa. It seemed an eon ago since she had stood in the yard at their farm, ready to battle with the strange man who had brought the news. She often wondered if she would feel better if they had let her get in one good swing.

She and Charley had taken the morning train to Papa's. It hadn't occurred to Emma until much later that she had missed her wedding. The more she apologized to Charley, the more he reassured her there was nothing to apologize for and that they'd get married as soon as Papa was well.

It was apparent to Emma that she couldn't leave Papa in Ida's care. Ida was a capable girl, but she was still a child. Ma couldn't care for him, and Lu had her hands full caring for Jackson, who'd had a run-in with one of his bulls. No, there was nothing to do but for Emma to stay.

Charley had gone home, promising to return as soon as he could arrange for someone to look after the farm. The problem was that he needed to harvest their wheat crop, but so did everyone else, so finding someone to mind the stock would be hard.

Doctor Perkins had told Emma that the apoplexy was most likely due to the arsenic poisoning Papa suffered at Matilda's hand. When Emma arrived, Papa had been in bed and looked very small and fragile. He didn't speak when she called his name, but he did seem to be trying to focus his gaze on her. She noticed his hand twitch a little and reached for it. Papa closed his eyes and slept for hours. Emma had sat there, holding his hand and praying that God would spare him. She didn't think that she could take losing him.

If he stirred, Emma would talk to him. She told him about all the grandchildren and her brothers and sisters in Caseyville. She told him about the farm that she and Charley were building, and she even told him about the strange man that she had almost attacked with her rolling pin. She would have sworn he smiled just a little when she described that.

The first week, Papa barely ate. If anyone except Emma tried to feed him, he'd refuse to open his mouth. Emma would spend all day spoon-feeding him persimmon tea that Ma had brewed. Ma said the tea would help keep his blood from getting too thick. Ida, Ma, and Widow Key offered to sit with him so that Emma could sleep in her bed, but as soon as she would lie down and close her eyes, someone would gently shake her, "Your papa needs you." While he didn't appear to be improving, he wasn't getting worse.

During the second week, Papa started talking again. At first, he made grunting noises. Emma quickly learned what each noise meant. She understood when he was too hot or cold when he was hungry, and when he was uncomfortable or in pain. Ida and Ma would try to relieve her, but as soon as Emma left the room, Papa would become fretful. Finally, they moved a cot into his room so Emma could lie down.

Letters from Charley and the family in Caseyville arrived almost daily. Her sisters wrote to reassure her that once she came back home, they'd see that she had her beautiful wedding. Charley wrote with news of the farm and harvest. They'd made a bumper crop of wheat, and he'd even been able to put back some seed for next year. As was their custom, the men went from farm to farm, cutting the wheat, and her brother, Albert, got it all to market at a tidy profit for everyone. Charley wrote that he had hoped to visit after the harvest, but one of the mares had foaled, and he needed to look after the colt for a bit. He described the baby to Emma and asked her to think of a name. She thought of all the "normal" horse names, but nothing seemed special enough for their first foal.

Emma read most of the letters to Papa and Ida. She hoped that hearing about the family would help Papa to heal. When she read to him about the farm where she and Charley would live, he would become agitated, so she stopped reading Charley's letters to him. Emma began to worry. What would they do if Papa never recovered? Ida couldn't take care of him even if he would allow it. At first, she thought that he could come live with her and Charley. That would be a lot to ask of Charley, to take in her invalid father just as they were getting married, but if he loved her…

She planned to write to Charley and ask if they could take her Papa and Ida, but the more she thought about that, the more she hesitated. Their home was large enough for the two of them, but with only one small extra bedroom, they didn't have room for two more people, especially when one was sick. She knew Charley planned to build more bedrooms upstairs, but could he afford to do it now?

Papa and Ida could live with one of her sisters, and she could go each day to care for him. That wouldn't be fair to

Charley, though. Betsy was the only one with enough room to take them in. Emma wouldn't have time for her own chores if she had to ride to Betsy's every day. The more she tried to figure out how to care for Papa and Ida, the more discouraged she became. It seemed the only option was for her to stay in Liberty Grove. She knew that the Bible said that she should honor her father, but did that mean she had to give up her own life?

Three weeks had passed, and Papa was making progress. His speech was close to what it had been, although he had to concentrate on the words at times. He sat in a chair on the porch several times a day and took short walks around the house. Ida would sit with him and sing, and Ma and Grandpa George would visit every few days.

Everyone's concern was beginning to shift from Ben to Emma. Even though he was feeling better and had his appetite back, Ben would only eat what Emma had prepared. Only Emma could fix his coffee; only Emma knew how to adjust the light blanket around his legs.

Grandpa George dropped Ma off on his way to town; she wanted to talk with Emma about when she planned to go home to Caseyville. Ben was napping in a chair on the porch, and Ma thought it would be the perfect opportunity to talk to her granddaughter. The women sat in the parlor, the window open, a light breeze fluttering the curtains. If Ben stirred, they'd be able to hear him. "Emma, have you thought about when you'll go home now that your papa is up and around?" Emma didn't answer right away, weighing her words carefully before she spoke. "Yes, ma'am, I've decided I should just stay here. With Papa having the problems he does and Ida still in school and too young anyway… maybe I wasn't ever supposed to go to Caseyville. Maybe I was always supposed to stay here with Papa."

Ma spoke slowly, "Emma, there's no reason for you to think that. Girl, you have a life, and a man who loves you is waiting there. It's time for you to head on home and start living. Things here will work out. Ben's doing better, Widow Key is more than happy to be here every day, and that boy of hers is doing a good job with the stock and chores. We'll all keep a watch and make sure that Ida doesn't have too much on her shoulders, but honey, it's time for you to get back to Charley.

He's been more than a little patient with all that's happened this past year. He deserves to have you there, sharin' his life, and you deserve to be there. Honestly, I think it's best for your papa if you leave. If you're here, he won't try as he should. Emma, he depends on you too much."

"Oh, Ma, I just don't know what to do! I miss Charley terribly and want to get married and start our life together. Our farm is so lovely, and the house that Charley built for us is a wonder. What if something else happens to Papa? It would be my fault! I've tried to think of a way to take care of Papa and be with Charley, but I can't see how. Maybe all the things that have kept me here are God trying to tell me this is where I'm supposed to be."

"Emma, you don't believe that for a minute, and neither do I. You're trying to take on a burden that's not yours to bear. Child, I love your papa, like my own son. The time we were apart after your momma died was a misery for me and your grandpa. Your papa hasn't been himself since Jane died, and he hasn't done right by his children. He let his grief steal all the love he felt and turn it into a sickness. Marrying that woman and allowing her to mistreat his babies was wrong. The only good to come of the whole mess was that dear, sweet Ida. Honey, you can't fix what ails your papa. He's better now that Matilda is gone, but what broke in him - only God can heal. Emma, you remind him too much of your momma, and if you let him, he'll keep you here till he dies, and you'll miss out on your own life."

Emma walked to the window to check on her Papa, and when she saw that his eyes were closed, she turned back to Ma, tears glistening on her cheeks. "Ma, I just don't know! I'm just so afraid that if I leave…" Ma interrupted her, "Emma, the longer you stay, the harder it will be to leave. Every day that you're here, your papa comes to depend more on you. Every day that you stay, he does less and less for himself. Be honest, Emma, if you weren't here, your papa would either let someone else help him if he needed it, or he'd find a way to do things for himself. Doc says he's doing fine now. He's eatin' good, talkin' plain, and can get around the place alone. If you're here, he's gonna sit in that chair and have you wait on him hand and foot."

Emma heard Papa stirring and quickly hugged Ma, "I'll think about it, and I'll talk to Papa about me going back to Caseyville. Maybe I could take the train next Friday?"

Chapter 15

Emma tried for two days to talk to Papa about her leaving. Whenever she brought up the subject, he needed her to check on how the stock was doing, bring him another blanket, or fetch his pipe. Once she would get him settled and try to bring up the possibility of leaving on Friday, she would look up, and he'd be napping. Her frustration was quickly growing.

When Thursday came around, and she hadn't made any progress, she announced that she was going to the mercantile. Maybe a brisk walk would settle her down. She had gone from being anxious about leaving Papa and something horrible happening to being downright angry that he had managed to thwart her every attempt to discuss the future. Emma had always been feisty and had a temper; she had worked up a full head of steam by the time she reached the mercantile. That caused her to send the telegram to Charley, saying she *would* be on the train arriving in Caseyville on Monday, July 15th. Exactly one month after the day that they were to have been married.

When she returned home, her temper had cooled, and she felt ashamed that she had stormed off. Ida was waiting for her on the porch, wringing the hem of her dress. "Oh Emma, thank heaven you're back. Papa is in such a state, and I didn't know what to do.", she wailed. Taking a deep breath, Emma marched into the house; it crossed her mind that she wished she had her rolling pin or a rock.

"Papa, what seems to be the problem?" Ben spoke slowly and carefully. "I'll not have a daughter of mine shaming herself by running after a man. Emma, you're too young to marry, and that man has no business trying to entice you at his age. Best you burn those foolish letters and put all this nonsense behind you. Write to your sister to pack your things and ship them back here, where you belong."

Emma's ears began to roar, and her heart began to pound. She knew that she needed to stay calm. She would make Papa understand that she was leaving on Monday and everything would be fine, *but she had to stay calm*, and she desperately wanted to scream.

"Papa, I understand your concerns and know you only want what's best for me. I mean no disrespect, but Papa, I <u>am</u> taking the train to Caseyville on Monday, and I <u>will</u> marry Charley. We have a farm and a home and <u>will</u> have a life together. Charley loves me like you loved Momma, and I love him. So, for the next few days, I'll see that everything is settled, including your care and Ida's, but come Monday, *I'm going home!*"

Ida pressed her back against the wall, trying to be invisible. She wanted to hear what they said but was terrified that Papa would notice her and be angry with her, too. She had never heard anyone talk back to Papa except her mother, and the last person she would have expected to do so was Emma. Papa's eyes narrowed as they faced off.

He started to speak, but Emma cut him off, "I'm very tired, Papa. I haven't slept well since I've been here, and I'm going to lie down now." With that, Emma turned and went to her room.

Ida stayed as still as a statue, not wanting Papa to notice her. She wasn't afraid of him, but she hated any un-pleasantness. She'd had enough of that when her mother was alive. Papa started to follow Emma, seemed to change his mind, and instead, went to the barn. Ida noticed that in his agitated state, he was walking normally instead of dragging his leg, as he'd done since his spell. She knocked softly on Em-ma's door when she was sure he wasn't returning. "Emma, may I come in?"

Ida wasn't sure what she expected to find her sister doing, but throwing her clothes into her travel case wasn't it. Ida noticed the letters scattered over the bed and the angry look on her sister's face. "Emma, I'm sorry, I didn't know what to do. Papa came out of your room, demanding to know where you were. He was stomping through the house and saying all kinds of things about how he never should have let you leave and that he would make you stay here, where you belong. Did he do that to your letters?" Emma looked at the letters that Charley had written her; Papa had read them and then crumpled them up. Emma was hurt and angry. Ma's words came back to her: *If you let him, he'll keep you here till he dies, and you'll miss out on your own life.*

Emma sank to the floor, head in her hands. How had her life gotten to be such a mess? She loved her family, especially Papa. She would never hurt any of them, but did making them happy mean she had to give up Charley? Ida sat beside her and placed her arm around her sister, "Emma, it will all work out. I know it."

The sisters sat, taking comfort from each other, until they heard the back door slam. Emma stood, smoothed her dress and hair, and walked out to face Ben. He was sitting in a chair by the fire, smoking his pipe, when she tried talking to him, he just closed his eyes and asked her for coffee. Fighting her frustration, she did as he  asked and sat quietly until he laid the pipe aside. "I'd like to talk to you about my return to Caseyville. You're doing so much better, and I would never leave if you *really* needed me here. Widow Key will be here to help, and it's still several weeks until Ida returns to school. Doc says you're doing much better than expected. It will be hard to leave, and I'll miss you all, but you and Ida could come to visit before school starts. I'd love for you to see the farm where Charley and I will live, and I know the rest of the folks would be thrilled to see you, too."

Ben rose awkwardly from his chair and walked to his room, dragging his leg again; he paused at the door and said, "Emma, I'm tired and don't feel right; best that you fetch the doctor."

Chapter 16

When Doc Perkins arrived, he examined Ben but could find nothing physically wrong. He said that it could be the after-effects of the poisoning or the apoplexy, or it could be something else altogether; Ben was getting up in years, after all. He had no fever; his eyes were clear, and his heart sounded strong. The doctor didn't have an answer for what was wrong. He'd check on him on Saturday, and in the meantime, they should keep him warm and comfortable and try to get him to eat. Emma asked the doctor to stop by Ma's and tell her what had happened. Then, she went in to check on Ben.

He was lying in his bed, looking very much as he had nearly a month ago when she had once again put her life on hold because he was ill. Emma knew she should be ashamed of what she was thinking, but she was angry and didn't care about what was right or Christian. She loved Ben and had tried to look after him for most of her life. She had done her best to make him happy and to protect him from Matilda, even when she didn't know exactly why he needed protection. Last summer, when Ben decided to send her to Betsy's, she had begged him not to make her go because she felt it was *her* responsibility to ensure *he* was safe.

He had insisted that she go. Not long after she arrived at Betsy's, she met Charley, and they fell in love. On the very night that Charley asked her to marry him, Ben was gravely injured in a fire. Emma had returned to Liberty Grove and spent months caring for him. It wasn't until Charley came for her at Christmas that they had been able to start planning their life together. Then, just two days before she was to marry, Ben had fallen ill again. Why was this happening? Was God telling her that her place was here with Ben? She didn't want to think about that. If she did, she would start to believe it; if she believed it, she would have to tell Charley that she couldn't marry him, and her heart *could not* stand that.

Ben didn't respond when she spoke, and Emma was ashamed of her thoughts and feelings when she turned and walked from his room. She should have sat with him, but her nerves were strung tighter than a piano wire, and it took all her self-control not to cry and yell at him.

Ma found her sitting on the steps. The old barn cat was curled at her side, and Emma's fingers absently ruffled his fur. Her eyes burned from fighting back tears. She didn't know what she would do about this mess she found herself in, but she wouldn't cry. She jumped when she felt a hand on her shoulder. She had been so lost in her misery that she hadn't heard anyone come outside.

Ma slowly lowered herself onto the step next to Emma. *When had Ma gotten old?* Emma had only been around her for a few months, but she could have sworn that Ma was nearly as spry as Ida last summer. *Was it all the extra work and worry of having Ben and Ida to look after?* It was obvious that Ma's role in caring for Ben would have to be limited to the medicines she prepared. Anything that required physical labor would have to be handled by someone younger and sturdier. Ida was too young, so once again, Emma concluded that she was the one who would be required to look after Ben.

The tears she had been fighting burned a trail down her cheeks; she could no longer hold them back. With a sob, she dropped her head onto her knees and let out all her anger and disappointment. Emma lost track of how long they sat there, Ma rubbing little circles on her back and whispering what Emma thought was a prayer. When her eyes were dry and her heart was empty, she turned to wrap her arms around Ma and kissed her cheek. "Thank you, Ma.

I appreciate you sitting with me. I had best get inside and check on Ida. I know she was pretty shaken up by all the unpleasantness earlier. I need to make sure she's all right and get some supper together." "Honey, I want you to sit here for a minute and tell me what happened between you and your Papa. Ida's fine: I checked on her. If Ben stirs and needs anything, she'll come to fetch us."

Emma told Ma about Ben reading her letters and forbidding her from marrying Charley. She told her grandmother that Ben was demanding she stay with him. After pouring her heart out to her grandmother, she was resigned to her fate.

Grandpa George had returned from town and was sitting next to Ben's bed when the women went inside. Ma took note of Ben's color and that he seemed to be clear-minded and felt well enough to smoke his pipe and take an interest in the local gossip that George was sharing with him. An uncomfortable thought crept in as she watched the exchange between the men.

Emma ran the back of her hand across Ben's brow and was pleased to find it cool. He seemed in better spirits, and she thought it was best to tell him what she had decided while Ma and Grandpa George were there; she hoped there would be no further upset. "I've been thinking about what you've said, and I'm going to send a telegram to Charley letting him know I won't be coming back. I'll go in the morning first thing." Emma swallowed the tears that threatened to fall; there would be no more; she would never be able to do this if there were more tears.

Ma noticed an almost sly smile cross Ben's lips and that his eyes shone ever so slightly. He said, "There's no need for you to do that. Just write what you need to say, and the Widow's son can take it for you." *So*, Emma thought *she would not even be allowed to send the message herself.* She wondered if this was what being in prison felt like. Ma patted her shoulder and said, "Emma, just jot down what you want to say, and your grandpa will take care of sending it."

Emma went to her room; she needed quiet to find the words to break Charley's heart. *Charley, I* ~~am so very sorry that~~ *can't marry you. My duty is here.* ~~No one else can take care of things.~~ *My*

~~heart is breaking.~~ ~~I pray that you find~~ ~~happiness~~. *Emma*

After neatly rewriting the message that would change her future, she folded the paper and pressed it to her lips. She would not allow herself to think of how Charley would react or of what she was losing. She would never be strong enough to see this through if she thought of those things.

Ma watched Emma closely as she walked back into the room and handed her message to her grandpa. She didn't think she had ever seen a more desolate soul in all her days. After hugging her granddaughters, Ma declared they best get home. Once they were away from the house, she told George to stop the wagon and give her the note. Ma read the carefully written words and knew

Charley would be as devastated as Emma. *This was wrong; it was plain to see that those two young 'uns belonged together, just as plain as it was that there was nary a thing wrong with Ben Jackson.* "George, you reckon anybody in Caseyville has one of those telephones?" George raised his brow as he looked at his wife, "Celey, what are you up to? You aren't figurin' to meddle in Emma's business, are you?"

Chapter 17

Emma's days were filled with caring for Ben. No one could do for him but Emma. Ida tried to help, but only Emma could do things correctly or fix his dinner how he liked it. Widow Key and her son stopped coming after the first few days; there wasn't enough work for them to do with Emma there.

In the mornings, she would settle Ben on the porch and head to the barn to milk and gather eggs. Some mornings, Ida would help her, but she preferred to be alone; it was the only time she wasn't under Ben's watchful eye. After she had told Ben that she would stay, she had carefully smoothed the wrinkles from Charley's letters and hidden them. She hadn't had the heart to destroy them as Ben had demanded. She had read each one and committed it to memory; in time, she might be able to think about the life she had lost, for now, it and the letters lay buried in the shade of a towering live oak tree.

Since the afternoon she had slipped away to bury the letters, Ben had kept her in his sight. There were times she felt she might suffocate. Once she committed to staying, Ben's health improved. If Emma went to the mercantile, he drove her in the wagon. When Ma and Grandpa came to visit, he stayed within hearing of the women. In the evenings, when she longed to go to her room and be alone, Ben wanted the three of them to sit in the parlor, the girls taking turns reading from the Bible. Emma was miserable and angry.

Ida's voice was soothing as she read, and soon Emma stopped hearing the words and was thinking about her family in Caseyville and how she missed them all. She wondered when or if she would ever see them again. Emma missed the evenings at Betsy's. After they cleared the table and put things to right, she and Betsy would sew or crochet while Doc caught them up on all the goings on in town. Their conversation had been filled with laughter, love, and plans for the future. It was almost time to put up jelly, and everyone would gather at Aunt Lucy's. The thought of working with those women whom she so dearly loved made her eyes prick with tears. She remembered last year and Aunt Lucy swatting Charley... she stopped that thought; she couldn't think of Charley.

Ben's voice dragged her back to the present. "Girl, are you ill?" "No, sir, I'm just a little tired. If you don't need anything else, I think I'll turn  in for the night." Emma closed the door to her room and buried her face in her hands, willing her head to stop throbbing. Thinking of her sisters and

Charley and the life they had planned together was something she could no longer afford to consider.

A routine had quickly developed, and Emma tried her hardest to be pleasant and not to resent Ben. She enjoyed teaching Ida how to cook and mend, and the truth was that Ida was what got her through each day. Emma had never known a sweeter girl than her little sister. Ida hummed constantly as if music bubbled up from her heart. She mostly sang hymns, knowing that some popular songs caused Emma distress. That morning, Emma had come in from gathering eggs and heard her sister softly singing,

"Absence makes the heart grow fonder
That is why I long for you
Lonely thro' the nights I ponder
Wond'ring darling if you're true
Distance only lends enchantment
Tho' the ocean waves divide
Absence makes the heart grow fonder
Longing to be near your side

Has the love that once was dearer
Than all else to me grown cold?
Or has absence drawn us nearer
To each other as of old?
Promise then, you will not sever
From the ties that bind us two
Say you will be mine forever
Tell me that you still are true"

Emma felt her heart shatter again as she thought of Charley. She wondered what he had named the foal he'd written to her about. She had meant to write that she would like to call him *Flash*. Silly, it hurt knowing she would never see the little horse. She physically shook her head as if doing so would dislodge the memories that threatened to spill down her cheeks as tears. Ida was still singing, and not wanting to distress her sister by walking in while she sang the ballad, Emma banged the door closed behind her.

Ida abruptly stopped her song and turned from the stove where she was cooking breakfast. Emma didn't appear to have heard what she sang; she wouldn't upset her sister for anything. She loved having Emma back home but knew her sister wasn't happy. She tried to help her in every way she could, thinking that maybe Papa would change his mind and let Emma marry Charley if he saw *she* was old enough to run the house and care for him.

She smiled as she placed a platter of fried eggs and bacon on the table and took hot, fluffy biscuits from the oven. A pot of coffee was brewed on the stove, and Ida set a glass of daisies in the center of the table. She patted Emma's arm as she went to call Papa.

Emma made a show of filling Ben's plate and pouring his coffee, not wanting him to hurt Ida's feelings by saying something wasn't quite right. Ida did *everything* the same as Emma, but to hear Ben tell it, *everything* tasted wrong unless Emma prepared it. It was a battle that she fought every day. As she prepared the plate of food, her mind drifted to the little farmhouse that Charley had built. She should be in their cheery kitchen with the window overlooking the pond cooking breakfast for Charley. It hurt that he had not even bothered to write to her. She knew she had no right to expect him to; after all, she had told him she wouldn't marry him with little explanation; still, she had hoped that he'd – oh, thinking of him wasn't helping! Her head was aching now, and there was a knot in her stomach. It had been three weeks since Grandpa had sent the telegram for her, and she had not heard a word from *anyone* in Caseyville.

After church the next morning, Ma invited them for dinner. Grandpa George told Ben he needed a good game or two of checkers, and Ben agreed they'd go. The ride to Ma's was quiet, and while they visited about the sermon and the local news over dinner, it wasn't like the boisterous meals at her sister's. Emma missed her family and how easily everyone joked and laughed as they prepared the meal and cleaned up. She thought about writing them and asking if they could come for a visit, but then she thought about how hard it would be to see them and not ask about Charley and how it would hurt when they had to go home, and she decided against it.

Ma asked Ida to run to the next farm to pick up some mending for her. Grandpa had been so busy he hadn't had a chance to take her, and she hadn't felt like walking. Emma started to volunteer, but Ma's look made her stay quiet. Ida was thrilled to help; she had heard that Ma's neighbors had a litter of puppies, and she secretly hoped to talk

Papa into allowing her to take one home.

Grandpa and Ben set up their checkerboard on the porch, and after they'd gotten caught up in their game, Ma motioned Emma to her bedroom. She softly closed the door, listened a moment then motioned for Emma to sit down. *Why is Ma acting so strange? Is there something wrong with her or Grandpa George?*

"Emma, I have something for you; you must keep quiet, though. That's why I sent Ida away, and your grandpa is distracting Ben." Emma couldn't imagine why Ma was so mysterious and wished that whatever her secret was, she would hurry and share it. Ma laid a finger to her lips and listened at the door for a moment more. When she was satisfied they wouldn't be disturbed, she drew a letter from the deep pocket of her apron. Emma's heart stuttered when she recognized Charley's handwriting.

Emma's hands were shaking so hard she couldn't open the letter. She pressed it into Ma's hands and whispered, "Please, Ma." When she finally held it, her tears could not be stopped as she read, "My Dearest Emma," in Charley's bold script. She had to read it several times before she grasped what Charley was saying. Her eyes flew to Ma's as realization sunk in.

"Honey, you've got to dry those tears and pull yourself together." Emma hadn't realized that she was silently sobbing as she reread the words that breathed hope into her heart.

"Emma, Ida will be back shortly, and Ben will be ready to get on home. Child, are you gonna be able to keep this secret? If Ben gets wind of what's afoot, I guarantee he'll have a spell of some sort. I hate to say such; I love him like my own, but honey, selfishness is the only thing wrong with that man. He misses your momma, and you remind him *so much* of her. He's had a hard road to travel, but it's one of his own making and not a bit harder than the one he made his children travel. Your grandpa and I love you, and we'll do whatever we can to help you. It's what my Jane would want for her baby girl."

Chapter 18

Emma prayed that she wouldn't give her secret away. The letter felt like a brand against her skin, where she had tucked it inside the waist of her skirt. She should have left it with Ma, but she couldn't. It was like a lifeline. How was she ever going to get through the next twelve days? She worried Ida was looking at her funny. *Did she suspect something?* She had to be careful, but not too careful, to act normal. Each day, she would do her chores as normal; that was the only way she could get through this.

Ben needed more attention than usual. *His coffee was cold; could she warm it? Could she help him with the chicken pen? Would she brew him some of that tea Ma made for his breathing?* Emma wasn't sure how much more she could take. Her nerves were about to the breaking point. She desperately wanted to take the letter to her hiding place, but Ben needed something else whenever she tried to escape. Too afraid to leave it in her room, lest he find it, she kept it tucked in her blouse, a constant reminder of all she had to lose.

It took almost a week to make her way to the oak tree. She kept telling herself to slow down, step carefully, don't run. Once, she was

certain she was being followed. Sweat beaded on her neck as she thought of an excuse for being so far from the house. Other than an outright lie, she couldn't think of a reason that would protect the secret she was guarding. When no one appeared, she hurried to the tree. After reading Charley's words again, she folded the letter, held it to her bosom, and breathed a silent prayer before burying it.

Emma's relief at seeing Grandpa George's wagon faded when she slipped back through the kitchen door and heard Ben say, "That girl is up to no good! I don't care what you say. She *is* hiding something, and I intend to find out what it is."

Emma's heart faltered; had she been careless? She stepped into the main room, hoping she didn't *look* guilty.

"Ma, Grandpa! I didn't know you were coming today. I went out to check the laundry and saw a patch of fleabane. Ida loves to have flowers on the table, and before I knew it, I'd wandered a good distance away. Let me put these in water, and I'll get us some coffee. Ma, is that an apple cake I smell?" Emma ducked back into the kitchen, saying a quick prayer of thanks for the handful of scraggly little flowers she had grabbed on her way home.

Ma and Grandpa George didn't stay long, but it gave Emma time to settle herself, and hopefully, Ben's suspicions had been put to rest. Emma suggested that they invite Lu, Jessie, and their families to dinner after church. Sundays were the most difficult days for her to avoid Ben and his gaze, which seemed to follow her every move. If the house were full of his children and grandchildren, he'd have less time to watch her. If Lu's oldest son, Riley, came with them, he would keep Ben occupied for the afternoon talking about his stock. Maybe she could suggest that Riley take his grandpa to see his horses one day next week? She silently blessed Ida for her enthusiasm about the family getting together, certain that was why Ben agreed.

Grandpa George came by on Tuesday to ask Ben's opinion about a fella he was considering taking on as a sharecropper. Grandpa said he was too old to keep up with more than a kitchen garden, but he didn't want the fields to go to weeds. He managed to make that conversation last more than an hour, and then Emma insisted he stay for dinner. Grandpa lingered over coffee, and he and Ben played checkers until Grandpa declared that "Ma would have his hide if he didn't get home." Emma walked him to the wagon and smiled when he gave her a conspiring wink before driving away.

By Friday, Emma thought her heart would burst from the strain. With Ma and Grandpa's help, she made it through the week with only minor scares. She desperately wanted to share her secret with Ida but couldn't take the chance of Ben discovering what she and her grandparents hid from him.

Emma went about her chores, taking special care with each task. The words from Charley's letter ran through her mind, *"rest assured; we will be married."* She forced herself not to think about tomorrow.

Ida had hovered near her all evening. She knew her sister suspected something, but Emma held her tongue. As much as she wanted to confide in her, she was thankful that Ida didn't press her.

Sleep eluded her. She tried to relax and then punched her pillow as if it was the reason she couldn't lie still. If she *didn't* lie still, she would wake Ben and have a mess to deal with. Just a few more hours; surely she could survive a little longer.

Emma lay in her bed and thought about the events that led to this moment. When she felt anger seeping into her thoughts, she started to pray. She figured she had a right to be angry but realized she was hurting herself by letting it control her. She asked God to forgive her for being angry and short with Ben. She prayed that God would heal the lonesomeness in Ben for Jane and help him see all the people who loved him and wanted to be part of his life. Her thoughts and prayers turned to Ida; she asked God to help her sister realize what a special young lady she was and help her follow His plan for her life.

Next, she prayed for Ma and Grandpa George. Emma thanked God for her grandparents and asked that He strengthen them and let her have them here on earth for a long time. Finally, she prayed for Charley. "God, I thank you for Charley and the life we're gonna make together. God, give him the words to say to Papa to help him see that this is *Your* plan for our lives and that just because I won't be livin' here doesn't mean I don't love him, and I'm not his little girl."

Emma then realized that the anger she had held so tightly was gone and that she felt peace about Papa for the first time in many years. Her eyelids fluttered then closed as she slipped into a dreamless sleep.

Chapter 19

The sun shining on her face woke Emma. She was shocked at how well she slept and thankful she rested for the first time in weeks. She listened for the sounds that meant Papa and Ida were awake. The house was quiet, so she slipped from the bed, planning to cook a special breakfast. She peeked into Ida's room, and seeing that she was still sleeping, Emma softly closed the door to let her rest for a while longer.

When Emma reached the kitchen, Papa drank his coffee at the table. She tried not to show her surprise, but this was the first time she had ever known Papa to get his coffee. She tried not to feel wary, but it was difficult; this wasn't normal behavior for him. "Morning, Papa. You're up mighty early. Give me a few minutes to gather the eggs and milk the cow, and I'll make your breakfast. We might have bacon *and* ham with our eggs this morning."

"Emma, sit down a minute." Her stomach flipped as she pulled out a chair and sat down. "Emma, I know you've been angry with me, and for that, I'm sorry. You must understand that I only want to protect you, and I know that you think you love this man, but Emma, you're still just a girl. It would be best if you trusted my judgment. The sooner you accept that I'm right about this, the sooner you'll stop this moping about."

She took a breath and then another. She silently prayed that God would give her the right words. She only needed to make it through a few more hours, and then Charley would be here. She wouldn't let her temper get the best of her. "Papa, I have been angry with you. I've asked God to take my anger away and forgive me, and now I'm asking you to forgive me as well. I was wrong to be angry when you only did what you thought was best."

Emma rose from her chair, and as she passed him, she bent and kissed her papa's cheek. She prayed that what she had said would forestall any further discussion. She felt that the less they talked, the better her chance was to keep him from discovering her secret. As she walked to the barn, she wished that Ma and Grandpa George were

there, but realized she couldn't hide behind her grandparents if she meant to be
treated as an adult.

Emma took her time cleaning up after breakfast. She washed and dried the
dishes and swept the whole house and
the porches. She fiddled with the furniture and moved a chair first, one place,
then another. She stood for a while and
gazed at the likeness of her parents that
once again hung over the fireplace.
Thankfully, Ben was in the barn looking after his horses; she would never
have made it through the day if he'd
been watching her. Emma went from
room to room, tidying the beds,
straightening the towels on the washstand, and counting every tick of the
clock.

Ida couldn't stand it any longer. "Emma, please, you must tell me what is happening. I know that something is wrong. I've tried to be patient, hoping you would tell me, but I can't stand this a minute longer!" Hugging her sister tightly, not knowing when she might see her again, Emma said, "Darling, I would tell you if I could. Nothing is wrong, but I can't tell you more right now. I love you, Ida; you're so special to me and have such a beautiful voice. Promise me that you won't ever stop singing."

When the clock struck noon, Emma almost jumped out of her skin. Only an hour more. Please, God, don't let the train be late. Papa came through the front door, wiping his hands on his handkerchief. "Girls, I thought we'd drive over to Runnels County and visit

Etta. It's been too long since we've seen them. Of course, with such a late start, we'll need to spend the night. We can stop by the Widow's place and ask her son to look after the stock." All the blood drained from Emma's face. *No! She couldn't leave. Charley was coming, and she had to be there. Papa knew! How had he found out? She had been so careful.*

She had to stay calm. She would pretend to be ill. That was dishonest, but her head started to pound, so it wasn't really a lie. Desperate to stall, she did her best to keep her voice from shaking as she said, "Papa, that would be lovely. I wish you'd have given me enough notice to bake something to take to Etta. I'll see what I might have and then wash up and change my dress. I got carried away with my cleaning this morning and got grimy." Emma hoped she could stall long enough for Charley to get there and prayed that, for once, the train would be early.

Emma walked from her room when she had taken as much time as she dared to change her dress and arrange her hair. She asked Ida if she was sure she didn't want to change her dress, too, but her sister must have missed the pleading look she gave her. She felt Papa's gaze on her and sighed as she gathered the baked goods to take to Etta. It was 12:45, and Charley's train wasn't due till 1. Even if it were on time, for once, it would be at least 1:30 before he got to the house. She had tried to think of a way to leave him a message. If Charley came for her and she wasn't there... she couldn't stand to think of that.

Papa helped them into the wagon and pulled out of the yard just as a buggy appeared over the rise. Emma's heart soared as she recognized Charley.

Chapter 20

Charley angled the buggy across the road to block the wagon. It wouldn't have surprised him if Ben kept driving when he realized it was Charley in the buggy. When he saw Emma, he felt like he could breathe for the first time in almost two months. He needed to get this mess sorted out, and then he and Emma needed to return to Caseyville, but not before he married her! Charley was going to ensure she was his wife once and for all. If she wanted a fancy wedding with her family, he'd see she got it when he got her home. In the meantime, a preacher in town could make things legal today, and he had the heavy gold band he'd bought for Emma tucked into his vest pocket.

Ben pulled his team up as Charley stepped from the buggy. He set the brake, told the girls to stay put, and stepped down. He sized the other man up as they walked away from their rigs. Ben wasn't young and had some illnesses, but he'd fight Charley if he had to. No one would ever say he didn't fight for what was his.

Ida climbed over the seat and clutched her sister's hand. She was afraid of what was happening. She wished Papa would return to the wagon and that Emma would make Charley leave. Emma realized she was holding her breath; she exhaled with a sigh. The only thing she knew to do was pray, and pray she did.

Ben said, "Now Charley, Emma told you she won't marry you. That's the end of all this nonsense. She's too young, and you're far too old to be looking in her direction. Best if you get back in that rig and go home and forget about my girl. My mind's made up, and Emma's not gonna disobey her pa." Ben started to walk away when Charley's hand shot out and grasped his arm. "Mr. Jackson, you've said your piece, but now I'll say mine. I love Emma, and I know that she loves me. We have a home we built together back in Caseyville, a home I plan to take her back to _today_. You say Emma is too young; if I recall correctly, her momma was only fifteen when you married her. Emma's closer to eighteen. I'd say she's plenty old enough to make up her own mind. If it weren't for looking after you, we'd be married already. Now, don't get me wrong. I'm glad she still has her pa, and I am happy for her to help, but Ben - Emma's place is with me, and *nothing* will keep her from me - not you or your "convenient" illnesses. By thunder, nothing else is keeping us apart. I'd appreciate your blessing, but trust me, we'll marry without it. You're welcome in our home, Ben, but *not* in our business."

Charley turned and walked toward Ben's wagon and his future. He helped Emma step down and stood staring at the face that was so dear to him. He looked up, noticing Ida for the first time. Charley reached up and took her hand. "Ida, I want you to know that no matter what happens, you are always welcome in our home, and you can come visit or stay anytime you would like." Emma smiled at her little sister and said, "I love you, sweetheart. I promise this isn't goodbye."

Charley helped Emma into the buggy, and as they pulled away, she heard Ben say, "You're no daughter of mine."

Chapter 21

11 Aug 1902

Emma couldn't believe that a year had passed so quickly. She and Charley had stopped at Ma's on their way to Liberty Grove. Ma held her tightly and said, "Now it's time for you and your young man to live your own lives." It had been hard to leave her grandparents behind. She'd had so little time to get to know them. Grandpa George promised they'd come for a visit, making it a bit easier to leave.

The drive to town was quiet. They were both thinking about Ben's final words. Charley considered whether he should turn around and take her back home, but he knew he could never leave her again. Emma's thoughts took a different direction. She was reminded of when Papa had told Ma to stay away after her momma had died. God had healed that rift; surely he could heal this one too. Emma just prayed it wouldn't take as long.

The preacher was waiting for them. Emma repeated the words he told her to, but it wasn't until Charley slipped the heavy gold band onto her finger and said, "With this ring, I thee wed." that everything be-came real. They were married, and they would be hus-band and wife  when they boarded the train. Charley kept apologizing to Emma about the hastiness of their wedding, promising that when they got back home, they could have another ceremony with all their family. As they sat, waiting for the train to depart, Emma stared at their joined hands and then looked into those blue eyes that had captured her heart from the first moment she saw them. "Charley, we're married now, and that's all I ever need." She started to look back down; what she needed to say next was difficult. Instead, she looked directly at him. "I'm sorry I've let Papa come between us and hurt you. I don't know why you came for me, but I'm sure glad that you did. I promise nothing will ever keep us apart again."

"Emma, when Ma called me, my heart…" "Ma *called* you! When? Was it after you got my telegram? Whatever did she say?" "Emma, slow down; I can only answer one question at a time. I never got your telegram; Ma didn't send it." Charley laughed, "She caused quite the uproar. Ma had Mrs. Eason call Driver's Mercantile in Caseyville. There were folks all over town looking for me. Clem found me at Uncle Frank's, and when he told me that I had a phone call from someone in Liberty Grove, I thought my heart would stop. I was scared half to death that you'd come to harm. When I got to the mercantile, folks from all over were waiting to see what was happening. I never got a telephone call; I wasn't even sure how to talk to the blame thing. Mrs. Driver had to show me how and kept telling me I didn't need to holler at it for Ma to hear me."

Emma giggled at the image of Charley yelling at the odd-looking box on the wall. Her curiosity aroused by what happened next, she gently nudged him when he remained quiet. "Anyway." Charley continued, "Ma said as how your pa had forbidden you from marrying me and how she suspected that he wasn't in as poor a state as he let on. She said that if I loved you, I had best hurry and come get you before it was too late. Ma told me you didn't want to stay, but you felt obligated. She said that was a bunch of hogwash and that it was time for you and me to get on with the business of living."

"Emma, I'm here to tell you that when Ma stopped talking, she left me with a heap of thinking to do. All the folks in the mercantile were naturally curious about what was happening, but

I needed time to digest everything. I rode Old Jumper to the pond where you fell in the water. I sat on that rock for hours and prayed about what was right for me to do. I came close to convincin' myself that I had no right to ask you to leave your pa, but then I got to thinkin' about all the plans you and me had made and the life we could have, and I knew, no matter what, I had to come and get you. At first, I was scared, thinkin' *What if she won't come back with me?* Then I just felt calm and peaceful. I decided right then that I'd be respectful to your pa, but I wasn't leavin' without you."

Emma was sure thankful that Charley had come for her. When they got home, her family insisted on celebrating with the whole community. Emma wrote to Ida and Ma, describing the festivities and letting them know that even though they weren't physically present, they were in her thoughts. She wore the lovely dress that her sisters had made for her with a tiny gold bar pin that Ma had given her at her throat, and with every step she took, she felt the faint impression of the "lucky" penny Ida had sent her inside her shoe.

Emma and Charley did "get on with the business of living." Emma's garden flourished, and Charley cleared another field to plant winter wheat. They saw their neighbors at church and enjoyed the get-togethers with family.

Ma and Grandpa George came to visit at Thanksgiving and even though Papa refused to come, he allowed Ida to. Ma brought Emma a cut-glass bowl that had belonged to her ma. Grandpa

George said Ma had carried it on her lap, wrapped in a quilt the entire train ride. It was  lovely having her little sister and grandparents with them; Emma was truly thankful for that blessing. Still, she missed Papa and prayed that he'd see his way clear to visit one day.

Christmas at Betsy's house was a joyous occasion. As Emma watched Uncle Frank, face beaming and a baby in each arm, she wondered if she would ever see Papa hold her children that way. Shaking off the wistfulness that threatened her happy mood, she smiled and patted Aunt Lucy's arm as the older woman hugged her and whispered,

"Have you told Charley he's gonna be a papa yet?"

From his place near the fire, Charley saw Emma's mouth form that perfect little "O." He made his way to her side, pushing down worry that something was wrong. This day was too perfect to be marred by anything bad. "Emma, honey, is something wrong? Did Aunt Lucy give you some bad news?" Her tears only worried Charley more; his thoughts flew to her family in Liberty Grove. *What has happened now?* Seeing the worry on Charley's face, she took his hand and led him outside; she had planned to tell him her news that night when they were alone at their farm.

Charley braced himself for the worst. It must be real bad if she couldn't tell him in front of the family. *What if something had happened to her pa? How could he ever let her go back there? How could he not let her go?* Emma watched the emotions as they flitted across Charley's face and was fascinated at how quickly they changed. When she saw the worry in his eyes, she knew she had to tell him now. "Charley, nothing's wrong, at least I don't think there is." For a moment, she was worried. *Would Charley be as happy as she was? They had talked about a family but had only been married a few months. What if he wasn't ready for children?* "Emma, please, just tell me what it is. Whatever it is, together, we'll handle it." Emma laid her hand on his cheek, hoping their baby would have his blue eyes. "Charley, you're gonna be a pa."

For a moment, Charley stood there in stunned silence. Before Emma could begin to fret, he let out a war whoop and twirled her around the porch. The commotion brought the family out to check on them, and as the happy news was shared, Emma was passed around for hugs and kisses while the men pounded Charley on the back in congratulations.

Ma and Ida wrote often, sharing the news of her family in Liberty Grove. They were both excited to hear about Emma's baby and that Agnes and Maggie were expecting little ones. Ma wrote that Emma's sister, Jessie, and her nephew, Riley's new wife, Della, were also expecting. Ma and Grandpa were doing well; they'd found a man to work the farm, and Grandpa was happy not working in his fields. Neither Ida nor Ma said much about Ben, and he hadn't answered any of Emma's letters. Emma prayed he was healthy and that, in time, he would forgive her for leaving. She hoped that one day soon, she would be allowed to introduce him to his grandchild.

Winter turned to Spring as Emma readied for their baby. She had knitted booties and little caps for the other babies that would soon join them and was working on a quilt for her little one with Aunt Lucy's help. She had decided on a butter-yellow material, and they were trimming it in cream. As her time drew near, Emma became more excited.

Emma couldn't remember a time when she had been this happy. Charley had finished their house and even built the baby a cradle, which waited for its tiny occupant in their bedroom.

Emma's hope chest held the tiny diapers and gowns she and her sisters had sewn. At least once a day, Charley would find her kneeling on the floor, the little garments spread around her as she gently held each one and imagined the day they would welcome their baby. As the baby grew, Charley often had to help her up from the floor; her chagrin at being "as big and clumsy as a house" only made him smile and love her more.

Emma had been blessed; she hadn't suffered from the morning sickness like poor Agnes; she had never felt more energetic. She continued to work in her garden, but canning her harvest proved the one thing she couldn't do. The vinegar smell turned her world *and* her stomach upside down. Charley hauled her garden produce to Aunt Lucy's, and the neighbor ladies helped her aunt with the canning, a kindness for which Emma would be eternally grateful.

Chapter 22

Emma was filled with wonder as her baby grew, and she felt little flutters and kicks from her womb. Her body grew heavy, her feet grew clumsy, and her energy ran out quickly. It was a warm day, late in the Spring. She was sitting in the porch's shade reading Ma's latest letter.

She loved hearing all the news from back home. She was grateful to hear that her grandparents had come through the winter with only a cold. They were both feeling quite well except for a touch of rheumatism. Grandpa had helped Ma turn the garden soil for the spring planting, and the next thing Ma knew, he'd taken over her garden. He missed working in his fields, even if he wouldn't admit it. Ma said that she was happy to let him have that chore. She had never cared that much for gardening once she moved to Texas. Trying to keep things alive in the heat was a trial. She wrote that she had plenty enough to keep busy without a garden to tend.

Ma wrote that Ida had a beau. Emma had difficulty thinking of her baby sister being old enough to have a young man call on her. Ma assured her it was just a passing fancy, but Ida was over the moon, and Ben had been hospitable enough. Emma felt a twinge of resentment but determined not to let it mar this momentous occasion in her sister's life. Still, it rankled some that Ida was only thirteen, and Papa wasn't objecting to the young man as he had Charley.

Emma missed Ma and wished that she could be here with her when the baby was born. She knew Betsy would be there and the doctor if she needed him, but having her grandmother there would be a comfort. She set the letter aside and dozed in her chair, as had become her custom in the afternoons. Charley often found her there when he came in from the fields.

Emma was having the most pleasant dream. She was sitting on her bed at Papa's, wearing her wedding dress. A shadow fell across her, and she looked up to see her momma and papa smiling at her. Momma walked to her, kissed her cheeks, and said, "Oh my baby girl, you look beautiful!" Papa smiled and chuckled, "That Charley is a lucky man." Emma started to speak, but her voice came out as a horrible squealing noise. She needed to talk to them, to tell them that she loved and missed them, but the only sound was squealing, and it grew louder.

She woke with a start and was on her feet and off the porch before she realized it. One of the hogs was loose and trying to get under the fence. If the blasted thing got under, Charley would never find it, and they needed to butcher that hog for winter. Emma thought he should have met his maker back in the winter at that moment.

If the beast got his head under the fence, she wouldn't be able to stop him from running off into the woods. In her haste to reach him, she hung her foot on a root, and the next thing she knew, she was flying through the air and landing face down on the hard ground.

Her first thought was that she couldn't breathe. The impact had knocked the air from her lungs, and try as she might, she could not draw even the tiniest bit in. She lay in the yard and began to take an inventory. She could wiggle her fingers and toes; she *thought* she could get to her knees. If she could crawl to the well, she could get a sip of cool water and pull herself up by holding onto the side. Lying on her stomach was uncomfortable, but she managed to turn onto her side and lay there a while longer, praying to feel a flutter.

Emma had hidden most of the evidence of her misadventure. Her hair was neatly combed, and she wore a clean dress. The scrapes on her palms were the only visible sign of her fall. The hog had made it to the woods, but that was the least of her concerns. It had been several hours since her fall, and she hadn't felt even the tiniest movement. She had started to go into town to the doctor, but it was too far to walk, and she was afraid to try to saddle a horse, much less ride into town. She contemplated walking down to Maggie's but was afraid to try even that short distance. She prayed Charley would hurry home, but the hours until he did felt like days.

Charley sensed something was amiss; his stomach churned with fear. Emma didn't rise to greet him as was her custom. As he washed the day's grime from his hands, he watched her face, hoping for a clue as to what she was keeping from him. "Charley, that boar got loose today. He rooted under the fence. I tried to get to him in time to stop him, but I tripped on something, and ..." Charley was beside her in an instant. She winced when he grasped her hands; he turned her palms up and saw the angry scratches. "Emma, what exactly happened?"

Charley thought his heart would burst as he raced to Maggie's. He couldn't bear leaving her alone but had to get help. Jim heard his yells and ran to meet him. He sent Charley back to Emma and headed for the doctor. Charley wished Maggie could go to her, but the shortcut between their houses was too rough for her to walk in her condition, and he couldn't bear to leave Emma alone long enough to fetch her in the wagon.

Charley was scared out of his mind when he returned to the house. He fought the terror he felt and whispered disjointed prayers. Emma was lying on their bed. She was curled in a ball as if trying to protect their unborn child. Charley noticed that she was clutching the little yellow quilt. He wanted very much to hold her but was terrified of hurting her. He pulled a chair alongside the bed and gently took her hand. He marveled at how small her hands were. He fetched the salve she kept for burns and carefully smoothed it over her palms. After what seemed a lifetime, Charley heard a buggy in the yard.

The doctor examined Emma, gently probing her swollen abdomen. After the exam, he told them she needed to rest in bed. She wasn't to walk around the house or sit in a chair. When

Charley asked if their baby was all right, the doctor replied, "Time will tell, son."

It had been two weeks since Emma felt her baby move. She begged God to let her baby be born healthy, but in her heart, she knew that it had died when she fell. Emma wanted to cover her head with the quilt and sleep. If she slept long enough when she woke up, this might all be a horrible dream. She caught Charley watching her, worry burning in his eyes. They hadn't been alone since the doctor left. Betsy had arrived, followed by her sister-in-law, Sallie, as the doctor drove away. One of them had been with her around the clock.

Emma was frightened. She was afraid because the baby wasn't moving, but she was also afraid that she would die. She couldn't find the words to tell anyone how she felt, so she silently poured her heart out to God. She wished more than anything in the world for Ma. If Ma was there, she just knew that everything would work out.

Late one night, Charley raced to fetch the doctor again. Emma was burning up and out of her mind with the fever. She had been feeling poorly for a few days. Betsy had told her that nature was taking its course, and her body was fighting against it. After waking the doctor, Charley pounded on the door to the mercantile. Mr. Driver swallowed the angry words he'd been about to heap upon the head of whoever woke him. He'd never seen anyone look as frantic as Charley.

Mrs. Driver promised to put a call through to Eason's in Caseyville and see to it that Charley's message reached Emma's grandmother.

Chapter 23

Emma delivered their son with the doctor's help and Charley by her side. Betsy washed her tiny nephew and wrapped him in the yellow quilt his momma and Aunt Lucy had so lovingly sewn for his arrival. Charley held his son and mourned what might have been if the little boy had survived. He placed the baby in Emma's arms for a few moments, then carried the tiny body to the coffin Doc and Jim had built.

Emma was too ill to attend the funeral, and they couldn't wait for her to recover to bury the child. Charley never dreamed that a heart could shatter into so many pieces and keep beating. He'd carved a cross to mark the grave;

when Emma was better, they'd give their son a name, and Charley would add it to the marker.

Four days had passed before Emma opened her eyes. She had never felt so weak and confused. Why was she in bed in the middle of the day? Blinking her eyes to adjust to the morning sun coming through the window, her first thought was that if she had died, heaven was a confusing place to be. Her papa was sitting next to her bed, head in his hands. Maybe this was a dream? She remembered a fever and horrible pain. There had been soothing words and someone placing cool rags on her brow. When she heard Ma's voice saying, "There's our girl.", she was certain that she was dead.

She struggled to sit up, but strong hands pressed her back into the pillows. "Emma, honey, take things slow." That was Charley's voice! If Papa, Ma, and Charley were all here, it was true she had died.

Her brow furrowed as she tried to re-member. *She had been napping, a noise startled her, something about a hog and running, then she'd had her breath knocked out... her baby!* Hot tears rolled down her face as her hand lay against her flat stomach. Her eyes sought Charley's, and what she saw there destroyed her. Charley held her in his arms until her last tear fell.

Feeling as if her body weighed a thousand tons, she pulled away from her husband. Nothing made sense. This had to be a horrible nightmare; if she could wake up, everything would be fine. "Here honey, you need to drink this." So, it wasn't a dream; that *was* Ma's voice. Emma remembered calling out for her when the pain was at its worst. She tasted something warm and slightly bitter but didn't have the strength to protest. When Ma removed the cup from her lips, she sagged back onto the bed, closed her eyes, and drifted into a fitful sleep.

It was dark when she woke this time. Her head hurt but felt clearer. She didn't open her eyes, listening for clues about who was in the room. Charley held her hand as he slept, slumped in a chair beside the bed. Quiet voices came from the parlor. Tired footsteps that had once been light as a cat approached the bed as Ma entered the room.

Ma saw her eyelids flutter and came to her side. "Can you tell me how you're feelin' darlin'? Are you hurting anywhere? Do you feel sick?" Emma's mind screamed, *No, she didn't feel sick, just weak. Was she hurting? How could she be when her heart had been ripped from her chest?* She whispered, "No, Ma, I'm better. Ma, is Papa here too?"

In the morning, Charley carried Emma to the porch. She insisted that she could walk, but he wouldn't hear of it, and Ma thought it best for her to take things slow. She sat for a time, her eyes closed, the sun heating her face. She was afraid to open her eyes, afraid to see the place where she had killed their baby. When she shivered, Charley carried her back to their bed, where she fell into a dreamless sleep.

As Emma grew stronger, Ma allowed her to get out of bed on her own and move about the house. She wandered from room to room and sat on the back porch that faced the barn, but Ma noticed she never went to the front porch or lingered at the kitchen window. Ma was pleased with her color and that her appetite was returning. Emma was sleeping less, but when awake, she was withdrawn, as if living in a separate world.

Ben waited for Charley to head to the barn and followed. Charley leaned against Old Jumper, rubbing the horse's neck and sobbing. Ben coughed before stepping inside, giving Charley a moment to compose himself. "That's a fine, strong-looking animal you've got there." When Charley didn't respond, Ben continued, "Charley, I owe you an apology. Son, there's no excuse for what I did interfering with the two of you. I'm not gonna make excuses. I was wrong in the head, but that wasn't a reason to try to keep you and my girl apart. I can see how much you care for her. It reminds me of how I felt about her momma - if you want the truth, how I still feel about her. Emma has always been a comfort to me; she's so much like my Jane. I didn't do right by my children, nary a one of them after their momma died. I cursed God and their grandma. None of that brought Jane or our baby back to me or our young'uns. I'm tryin' to say, don't let this tragedy build a wall between you and Emma. I know my girl; she takes on the world's weight, and right now, she's faultin' herself for what happened. I'm countin' on it that you're a better man than me. Don't let this wound fester and poison your heart. Don't let it steal the precious time you have together. I heard you talking about how you should have killed that hog sooner, and none of this would have happened. Truth is, there's nothin' you could have done; life happens the way it does, and we don't always get to know the why of it. It sure ain't your fault any more than hers. Right now, you're both plumb eat up with blamin' yourself and what ifs. Instead of grieving together over what you've lost and healing, you're both closed off in your private sorrow. Son, that's not the way. Listen to an old man who wasted his life disparagin' the folks he loved the most, and that loved him. Now, that's the longest piece I've spoke in a good while. You pray on it, and then you go to your wife. She's miserable thinking she's let you down."

Charley sat in the shadows on a hay bale, mulling over Ben's words and talking to God. He'd never cared much for Ben. The man had caused him a lot of aggravation the past year. He tolerated him because Emma loved her pa, and Charley loved Emma. Ben's words had struck their mark, though. He *was* blaming himself; he was supposed to protect Emma and their children, and in his mind, he had failed, but in wallowing in his self-loathing, he was hurting his wife, which he couldn't bear. It's funny the ways God used to get through to His children. Charley reckoned that if the Lord could make a donkey talk to get His point across, He could use an old man with more than his share of heartaches.

Chapter 24

Emma walked into the barn; she needed somewhere quiet to think. She knew that Charley must hate her. It was her fault that their baby had died. His son would be alive today if she hadn't been so careless. If only she could make him forgive her, how could she even ask him to when she couldn't forgive herself?

Charley heard her soft weeping and went to her side. He wanted more than anything to hold her and to take the pain she was feeling from her. He reached to touch her face and hesitated, unsure how she would react, terrified that she would turn away. He shoved his hands into his pockets and stepped back,

afraid to speak, more afraid to stay silent. Ben was right; he needed her, and
she needed him. If only he weren't terrified that she would never forgive him.
He thought of the Bible verse in Isaiah:
*"Fear thou not; for I am with thee: be
not dismayed; for I am thy God: I will
strengthen thee; yea, I will help thee."*

"Emma, do you feel up to a little
walk? If you start to feel tired, we can
turn right around." Suddenly, a walk
sounded wonderful. She had lost track
of how long she had been confined to
the house and the porch. Emma knew
she had come very close to dying and
that Ma and everyone else was concerned about her, but the constant
watching and fussing was taking a toll.
Not trusting her voice, she walked from
the barn, looking back at Charley, praying that he would understand and

follow.   Charley led the way, picking an easy path and walking slowly. They walked silently, not ready to speak what was in their hearts. Before long, they realized that they were nearing the pond and were shocked at how far they'd come. The ground was uneven, and Charley lightly grasped Emma's arm to steady her, releasing his hold as soon as the path was smooth again. Emma re-gretted that he moved his hand away. For a moment, she had felt safe, as if her world might one day be right again. She was suddenly very tired. Memories of the first time she had seen Charley here and the night they'd sat in his buggy on the rise above flooded her heart with emotions.

Emma sat on a rock, staring out over the pond. She wanted to say so much but didn't know where to start. Charley watched in misery, seeing the sadness in her eyes and praying for a way to wipe it from them and her heart. In a moment that he later would say was divine inspiration, he picked up a rock and placed it in her hand.

Emma looked from the smooth stone in her palm to Charley; his blue eyes glistened with tears. He spoke quietly and reverently: "We got off to a rough start right here more than a year ago. When I first saw you standing there, I thought you were the loveliest vision I'd ever seen. I thought I was dreaming, but then you..." Charley smiled and rubbed his cheek exactly as he had back then.

Emma leaned her head against his shoulder, the contact giving her the courage to speak. "I only threw it at you because you were rude." Charlie heard the faint smile in her voice as they remembered that day, which seemed eons ago. "Well, you reckon if you whacked me with another one, we'd both feel better?" Emma's tears came in a torrent as she turned into his arms. By the time they started back home, the sun was going down, and they'd talked about the guilt and anger they'd each felt and about how they each had felt responsible for the death of their baby boy. They mourned their loss, offered and accepted forgiveness, and promised never to shut the other out again, no matter what they faced. They talked about everything they'd been through in the past year and even began to talk about their future. Charley asked her if she wanted him to move the cradle to the attic, and after a moment, Emma told him that if it were alright with him, she would rather keep it where it was as a reminder of God's love and promise.

Ma and Ben were sitting on the porch and watched as Emma and Charley made their way to the little grave under the oak. Charley had insisted that they bury the baby on the farm where they could watch over him. Emma knelt and caressed the cross Charley had carved. She looked up at Charley and nodded. As the sun sank in the west, Charley knelt beside her, took out his knife, and carved –

Charley Henderson, Jr.

May 1902

Epilogue

12 July 1904

Emma's hand trailed over the shabby coat with the faded green patch that hung in the shed room. It had belonged to the man who brought the message about her papa's illness years earlier. Emma had fainted from stress and shock, and it wasn't until much later that Charley had noticed the discarded coat.

Her memories of the strange man and Papa's illness were easier to live with now, although she could still feel her terror when she thought of that day. Charley had left the coat hanging by the well for a time. He'd asked their neighbors about the man, but no one knew him. Eventually, he'd hung the old coat in the barn. Emma had started wearing it one morning when she went out to gather eggs and forgot her coat. Since then, it had hung in the shed room. When she wore as she gathered eggs or did the milking, she often wondered about the man, where he had come from, and where he had gone.

As she stepped from the shed into her kitchen, Emma smiled into the up-turned face of the little girl. She had never felt love this strongly. When Alta was born, Emma kissed each of her tiny fingers and toes, marveling at the wonder of creation. Charley had been beside himself, crowing like a rooster over the birth of their baby girl. To hear him tell it there had never been a prettier or sweeter baby than his little girl.

Alta sat in the middle of the brightly colored rug in a dress that Betsy had sewn. Her orange cat, Rudolph, was pouncing on her doll. Alta had forgotten her dolly when her daddy had fastened a tiny gold bracelet around her chubby little wrist. Emma had scolded Charley briefly, but he insisted that his girl needed a "pretty" for her first birthday.

Emma whipped cream into the frosting for the coconut cake she had baked knowing it was Charley's favorite. Cookies for the children were cooling on the table. Through the open window, she could hear wagons pulling into the yard and the sound of laughing children mixed with the adults calling out greetings. The entire family was coming for Alta's first birthday celebration. Emma laughed when she thought about the party for the little girl. She had told Charley that making such a fuss over a baby was silly. She tried telling him Alta wouldn't care if she had a party. Her words fell on deaf ears, and in the long run, they had all gotten caught up in his excitement, and so, today, for the first time in many years, all her siblings and their families, as well as all of Charley's family, were gathering to celebrate.

A soft knock preceded Ma's faltering step into the house. Emma realized how blessed she was to still have her grandmother. She hurried to help her to the rocker and watched in delight as Alta crawled across the floor and pulled up to be held by Ma.

Ma was there when Alta was born. Emma watched as her elderly grandmother cuddled her little girl and whispered secrets in her ear. Alta's little hands patted Ma's wrinkled face as she babbled secrets of her own. Emma had begun to believe that they understood what the other was saying - so close was their bond.

Soon, the yard was full of makeshift tables covered with food. Babies were passed from arm to arm as mothers prepared plates for their children and kept an eye out for mischief. Alta was sitting on her grandpa's lap, trying her best to help him with his chicken leg. Ida offered to take her niece, but Ben was not about to surrender his prize.

It was hard to understand how much had happened in just over a year. After Emma and Charley's baby had died, Ben had made peace with Charley, and he, Ida, and her grandparents had been to visit several times. When Alta was born, Papa had come to meet his newest granddaughter as soon as he could catch a train to Caseyville. He'd stayed a week, visiting all the folks, and when he left for home, it was with a promise to visit again soon.

There had been great sorrow and joy along the road they had traveled; hearts had broken and mended, lives had ended, and others had begun. As Emma looked around at the people she loved, Charley handed her a rose from one of the bushes she had planted, took her hand, and whispered, "Emma, I sure am thankful you can chuck a rock. I would have hated to miss out on this life of ours."

Emma laughed, and as she turned to lay a hand on his cheek, she realized that God had blessed her with all she had ever dreamed of and that no matter where the road ahead might lead

- love was all that mattered.

Characters

The Cooper Family

Jackson - *husband of Luella Jackson*

Riley - *son of Jackson Cooper and Luella Jackson, brother of Ebb and Sam*

Ebb - *son of Jackson Cooper and Luella Jackson, brother of Riley and Sam*

Sam - *son of Jackson Cooper and Luella Jackson, brother of Riley and Ebb*

The Dobbs Family

Celey - *"Ma," widow of Daniel Tilman, wife of George Marcus, mother of Jane Tilman*

The Foster Family

Doc - *son of Frank and Lucy (Whitaker) Foster, married to Elizabeth "Betsy" Jackson, father of Jane and Victoria.*

Frank - *"Uncle Frank," married to Lucy Whitaker, brother of Clara and Sarah, father of Doc, Jim, Sallie, and Samuel, uncle of Ben Jackson and Charley Henderson*

Jim - *son of Frank and Lucy (Whitaker) Foster, married to Margaret "Maggie" Jackson, father of Jesse, Ed, Ada, and Ben*

Sallie - *daughter of Frank and Lucy (Whitaker) Foster, married to Amos Jackson,*

The Henderson Family

Alta – *daughter of Charley and Emma (Jackson) Henderson, sister of Charley, Jr.*

Charley – *nephew of Frank and Lucy (Whitaker) Foster, husband of Emma Jackson, father of Charley, Jr. and Alta*

Charley, Jr. - *son of Charley and Emma (Jackson) Henderson, brother of Alta*

The Jackson Family

Agnes - *daughter of Ben and Jane (Tilman) Jackson, sister of Luella, Elizabeth, Silas, Margaret, Albert, Thomas, Jacob, Amos, Jessie, Emma, and Ida, married to Samuel Foster, mother of Claire*

Albert - *son of Ben and Jane (Tilman) Jackson, brother of Luella, Elizabeth, Silas, Margaret (twin sister), Thomas, Jacob, Agnes, Amos, Jessie, Emma, and Ida*

Amos - *son of Ben and Jane (Tilman) Jackson, brother of Luella, Elizabeth, Silas, Margaret, Albert, Thomas, Jacob, Agnes, Jessie, Emma, and Ida, married to Sallie Foster*

Ben – *son of William and Sarah (Foster) Jackson, widower of Jane Tilman, husband of Matilda Seward, father of Luella, Elizabeth, Silas, Margaret, Albert, Thomas, Jacob, Agnes, Amos, Jessie, Emma, and Ida*

Elizabeth – *"Betsy," daughter of Ben and Jane (Tilman) Jackson, sister of Luella, Silas, Margaret, Albert, Thomas, Jacob, Agnes, Amos, Jessie, Emma, and Ida, married to Doc Foster, mother of Jane and Victoria*

Emma - *daughter of Ben and Jane (Tilman) Jackson, sister of Luella, Elizabeth, Silas, Margaret, Albert, Thomas, Jacob, Agnes, Amos, Jessie, and Ida, wife of Charley Henderson, mother of Charley, Jr. and Alta*

Ida – *daughter of Ben and Matilda (Seward) Jackson, half-sister to Etta McDowell and Luella, Elizabeth, Silas, Margaret, Albert, Thomas, Jacob, Agnes, Amos, Jessie, and Emma Jackson*

Jessie - *daughter of Ben and Jane (Tilman) Jackson, sister of Luella, Elizabeth, Silas, Margaret, Albert, Thomas, Jacob, Agnes, Amos, Emma, and Ida, married to Henry McDougal*

Luella – *"Lu," daughter of Ben and Jane (Tilman) Jackson, sister of Elizabeth, Silas, Margaret, Albert, Thomas, Jacob, Agnes, Amos, Jessie, Emma, and Ida, married to Jackson Cooper*

Margaret – *"Maggie," twin of Albert, daughter of Ben and Jane (Tilman) Jackson, sister of Luella, Elizabeth, Silas, Albert, Thomas, Jacob, Agnes, Amos, Jessie, Emma, and Ida, married to Jim Foster, mother of Jesse, Ed, Ada, and Ben*

The McDowell Family

Etta – *daughter of Matilda (Seward) and Mr. McDowell, half-sister of Ida Jackson, wife of James Miller*

The Marcus Family

George – *husband of Celey "Ma" (Dobbs) Tilman*

The Miller Family

James – *husband of Etta McDowell, father of Lee and Jim*

Lee – *son of James and Etta (McDowell) Miller, brother of Jim*

Jim - *son of James and Etta (McDowell) Miller, brother of Lee*

The Seward Family

Matilda – *widow of Mr. Hadley, ex-wife of Mr. McDowell, wife of Ben Jackson, mother of Etta McDowell and Ida Jackson*

The Tilman Family

Jane – *daughter of Daniel and Celey (Dobbs) Tilman, married to Ben Jackson, mother of Luella, Elizabeth, Silas, Margaret, Albert, Thomas, Jacob, Agnes, Amos, Jessie, and Emma*

The Whitaker Family

Lucy – *"Aunt Lucy," married to Frank Foster, mother to Doc, Jim, Sallie, and Samuel*

Caseyville Residents

Mr. and Mrs. Driver

Mr. Hogue

Clem Kincaid

Ed Simmons

Grace Webb

Liberty Grove Residents

Doctor Perkins

Mrs. Eason

Widow Key

Coconut Cream Cake

Heat oven to 375°F.
Bake for 25 minutes in four (4) greased, 9-inch round layer (cake) pans.

Ingredients

4 – cups Swan's Down Cake flour, sifted (any cake flour is fine)
2 – teaspoons baking powder
1/4 – teaspoon salt

1 – cup butter

2 - cups sugar

6 – egg yolks, well beaten

1 – cup + 2 teaspoons milk

2 – teaspoons vanilla

6 – egg whites, stiffly beaten (save 4 yolks)

Instructions:

Sift flour once, measure, add baking powder and salt, and sift together three (3) times.

Cream butter thoroughly, add sugar gradually, and cream together until light and fluffy.

Add egg yolks, then flour (dry mixture) and milk – alternately – a small amount at a time.

Beat after each addition until smooth.

Add vanilla and fold in egg whites.

Pour equal amounts into four (4) cake layer pans and bake in a moderate oven (375 degrees) for 25 minutes.

Put layers together with Coconut Cream Filling and cover the sides and top of the cake with Coconut Butter Frosting.

Coconut Cream Filling

1 – cup Swan's Down Cake flour, sifted (any cake flour is fine)

1 ½ - cups sugar

¼ - teaspoon salt

4 – cups milk, scalded

4 – egg yolks, well beaten

2 – teaspoons vanilla

1 ½ - cups Baker's flaked coconut

Instructions:

Combine flour, sugar and salt.

Gradually stir in milk, then place in a double boiler and cook until thickened, stirring constantly.

Pour a small amount of hot mixture over egg yolks and stir until mixed well; add back to double boiler and cook 10 minutes longer.

Stir in vanilla and coconut.

Cool and spread between layers of Coconut Cream Cake.

Coconut Butter Frosting

Ingredients:

1 – cup butter

2 – cups confectioners' sugar

8 - Tablespoons cream

1 – teaspoon vanilla

3 – cups Baker's flaked coconut

Instructions:

Cream butter, add sugar slowly, and cream until light and fluffy.

Thin with cream as the mixture becomes stiff.

Add vanilla.

When frosting is the consistency of whipped cream, spread on Coconut Cream Cake and sprinkle it with flaked coconut.

Other Titles Available

<u>Fiction</u>

Emma: Heritage Series- Volume I

A real-life Cinderella story - complete with a wicked stepmother. - "Emma lay very still, her eyes tightly closed. Sometimes - if she concentrated - she could make out her Momma's face. She was the youngest child of eighteen. She had barely been two when her beloved Momma died. Losing Momma had hurt Papa deeply. No one had wanted him to be sad, but why did *she* have to be their new mother?" Based on the author's great-grandmother and events in her life, much of the story is fiction. However, threads of reality are woven throughout Emma's story. The real-life Emma was the youngest in a family of eighteen children. As to the rest, it is up to the reader to decide, fact or fiction.

Lone Star Literary Life Review

"It wasn't age or distance that mattered – love was all that mattered."

"Emma by Susan Diane Black Blackmon is the first in the Heritage Series. With a strong historical foundation, this fiction flows like a traditional fairy tale that has both dark and light elements, providing readers with an early 1900s Texas narrative, a sweet romance, and an evil stepmother.

Blackmon's writing style is clean and uncomplicated, making Emma an ideal choice for readers of all ages, including middle-grade and young adult readers who enjoy an interesting Texas fiction based on real-life people and events.

Emma can rightly be likened to Cinderella. However, this story resembles Little House on the Prairie by Laura Ingalls Wilder as well, with the very act of survival in a harsh land during a harsh time providing more than enough turmoil, hardship, and even celebrations, such as box socials and courtship. Add a woman who chooses to destroy others to satisfy her avarice, and Emma quickly becomes a modest yet powerful parable and cautionary tale. Rising above and even overcoming wickedness will always resonate with readers as relatable and meaningful, with Blackmon nimbly delivering the effective trope of good versus evil and so much more in this first fascinating book in the Heritage Series."

"This was such a heartwarming read. As the description states, it's based on a Cinderella-like story, but there are many more layers to this story. You won't regret this one!"

"Loved the story....had a hard time putting it down...I am looking forward to the next edition."

<u>*"This book kept me wanting to know what was going to happen next.*</u> *Emma made me laugh and cry. I read it in one day. I cannot wait to read the next book."*

"I am delighted how the story was a page-turner and hard to put down. Emma's story is very heart-warming and real-life Cinderella indeed. The details

of the narrative are on point as well. I love this one very much."

Celey: Heritage Series – Volume II

When Celey Dobbs met Daniel Tilman, was it chance or God that brought them together in the unsettled region of Scott County, Arkansas?

We first met Celey in the story of Emma, her granddaughter. Now, join Celey and her family as they journey through the untamed prairies of Illinois, the violent beginnings of the state of Arkansas, and the wild frontier of Texas.

Celey's story is based on letters written by the author's maternal great-great-

great-grandmother, detailing events in her life.

"A slow rain fell as Celey walked from the graveyard, her tears mingling with the tears of God.

In the distance, she saw Tom Anderson. Her heart raced, and her anger flared. How dare that rotten scoundrel show his face here!"

Much of the story is fiction, but as always, threads of truth are woven through the tapestry. It is up to the reader to decide what is fact and what is fiction.

Lone Star Literary Life Review

"The land was good; the vermin that dwelled there were not."

Celey by Susan Diane Black Blackmon is the second book in the Heritage Series. This continuing fiction is steeped in rich familial history and written for all ages to enjoy. The first book, Emma, highlights the story of Emma Jackson, who is the daughter of Jane Tilman and granddaughter of Celey Dobbs. While the books in this series can stand alone, they are better together because they show how life in the late 1800s and later was fraught with hardship, illness, and murder, but also filled with love, family bonds, hard work, and hope.

After a brief historical introduction, Celey begins on a dramatic note, with the villainous Tom Anderson harassing young Celey Dobbs and her little sister in the mercantile in Waldron, Arkansas, in Scott County. Anderson wants to buy the prime land in the county and is full of revenge and bedevilment when some families refuse to sell, including the Dobbs family. This scene in the mercantile sets the stage for the entire book, with Anderson remaining a savage thorn in everyone's side, and with Daniel Tilman rescuing young Celey from Anderson's clutches and losing his heart to her in the process. The rugged land and daily toils are difficult enough without having a crooked sheriff in Tom Anderson's pocket. Despite the corruption and constant threat, the entire community is determined to fortify their small town and surrounding farms with a church and a school and come together to thrive and grow.

Blackmon quickly lures the reader into Celey's sojourn as a daughter, sister, wife, and mother in Arkansas and finally in Texas. The network of families in Celey portrays a microcosm of life in the late 1800s in a severe yet innovative environment, including the start of the Common School Law, the irresistible call of the California Gold Rush, and the promise of fertile land and a better life in Texas for ranchers, farmers, and cowboys. Blackmon deftly juxtaposes the heartbreaking reality of losing children, spouses, and other family and friends with the joy of social gatherings, worship, and camaraderie among relatives and neighbors alike.

This fiction is Christian based and tightly reinforced with a strong historical foundation and the day-to-day challenges, failures, and successes of regular folk trying to eke out a living reminiscent of Laura Ingalls Wilder's Little House on the Prairie series. Blackmon presents readers with a cherished gift in this Heritage Series because the simple tales of these characters will transport readers back to a time when much of the country was still wild, untamed, and dangerous, yet beautiful and full of promise and adventure.

The pacing is steady, with the occasional dramatic and even startling spike mixed with the prosaic activities to keep readers engaged and entertained. Several sketches throughout offer interesting glimpses into the interworking of Celey's amazing story, and a few recipes, such as cold biscuit puddin' and brandy sauce, at the end will entice readers to try some pioneer fare. Through such an engaging historical fiction, the people, both good and evil, in Celey and the entire Heritage Series will surely encourage readers to research their own family history or simply acknowledge the contributions and sacrifices of those who valiantly forged new paths across a rough and daunting frontier.

"Loved this book...just like I did Emma...when I first started reading on it...read 7 chapters before I knew it...looking forward to book 3...highly recommend both books"

"Celey's story is captivating - a page-turner and entertaining to read."

Self-Publishing Review, ★★★★

Self-Publishing Review, ★★★★

"Celey by Susan Diane Black Blackmon is an American historical fiction novel set in the nineteenth century.

Blackmon transports readers back in time to a family, not unlike many of our own. Celey's story is one of persistence, faith, and the unyielding American spirit that keeps hope alive, even in the darkest of times. Her story weaves a wondrous tapestry of love and loss, pain and redemption, family and lasting friendships.

Blackmon instantly pulled me into the story of Celey, and before long, I felt as if her story was a glance into my story as well! Her family wasn't wealthy, but they were rich in love and had everything they needed, all provided by God. I loved the simple way of life, portrayed here as not lacking, but natural and full of unexpected blessings. This is a story of great pain and greater restoration as her family weathers the storms of life. The firm bonds of friendship and community that only grow stronger as the family draws closer is a beautiful testament and one I felt strongly throughout Celey's story. Celey is a heartfelt and poignant story that's impossible to put down and sure to delight readers!"

It is an engrossing and evocative work of historical fiction. Blackmon's research on daily life in 19th-century Arkansas provides a remarkable backdrop to Celey's story, which feels as immediate as a contemporary story. The nuances of Celey's feelings make the reader ache for all her troubles while admiring her strength, creating a multilayered character and an emotionally complex reading experience. Well-written, historically accurate, and vividly emotional, this heart-wrenching piece of historical fiction is an unforgettable novel."

<u>Nonfiction</u>

The Giles Driver Family
A Compilation of the Descendants of Giles Driver
Isle of Wight, Virginia
Volume I

CREDCREDCREDCREDCREDCREDCRED

The Giles Driver Family
A Compilation of the Descendants of Giles Driver
Isle of Wight, Virginia
Volume II

CREDCREDCREDCREDCREDCREDCRED

Whispers from the Past…..
Buytenhuys to Boultinghouse
Volume I
Immigration, Canadian Kin, & Migration

CREDCREDCREDCREDCREDCREDCRED

Whispers from the Past…..
Buytenhuys to Boultinghouse
Volume II
The Descendants of Daniel Boultinghouse 1797-
1867

ↄ℈⅁ↄↄ℈⅁ↄↄ℈⅁ↄↄ℈⅁ↄↄ℈⅁ↄↄ℈⅁ↄↄ℈⅁ↄ

Daniel Brown Boultinghouse
&
Mary Jane Russell
A Collection of Civil War Letters
and
Family Documents
With Genealogical and Historical Commentary

ↄ℈⅁ↄↄ℈⅁ↄↄ℈⅁ↄↄ℈⅁ↄↄ℈⅁ↄↄ℈⅁ↄↄ℈⅁ↄ

For more information, contact:
Susan Black Blackmon – 940-550-8322

whispersfromthepast.net
grandmastrunk.net

Author's Amazon Page –
https://www.amzon.com/~/e/B07GTPTC2H

Illustrations

Page 3 – iStock.com/Natastic

Page 19 – iStock.com/KenWiedemann

Page 22 – iStock.com/Pimpay

Page 29 – iStock.com/whitemay

Page 39 – iStock.com/Luisa Vallon Fumi

Page 61 – iStock.com/Campwillowlake

Page 67 – iStock.com/ilbusca

Page 91 – iStock.com/Pimpay

Page 105 – iStock.com/Pimpay

Page 129 – iStock.com/Nastasic

Page 161 – iStock.com/KenWiedemann

Page 176 – iStock.com/Beeldbewerking

Page 188 – iStock.com/clu

Page 255 – iStock.com/ilbusca

Page 259 – iStock.com/Maksim-Manekin

Page 178 - *Absence Makes The Heart Grow Fonder*
– Lyrics by Arthur Gillespie, 1907